Blanche

A cat's tale of love, loyalty
and betrayal

Blanche

A cat's tale of love, loyalty and betrayal

Brenda Harrison

First published 2020

Published under licence by Brown Dog Books and
The Self-Publishing Partnership, 7 Green Park Station, Bath BA1 1JB

www.selfpublishingpartnership.co.uk

ISBN printed book: 978-1-83952-244-4

Cover design and illustrations by Andrew Prescott
Internal design by Tim Jollands

Printed and bound in the UK

This book is printed on FSC certified paper

For Blanche and Lucy

Contents

A Bit of Background

Blanche is a nine-year-old Siamese cat and she lives in Wells, the smallest city in England. Wells is in the county of Somerset and is a bit of a tourist attraction because of its many outstanding historical buildings. But these famous historical sites do not impress Blanche. In her opinion, no other place in Wells holds more charm and interest than her own home in Overwood Close.

Estate agents describe Overwood Close as a 'sought-after location' because it is so private, yet it is only a short distance away from the shops on the High Street. It branches off a steep rise of detached, chalet-type houses called The Avenue. Overwood Close itself is a leafy cul-de-sac made up of six more detached chalet-type houses.

Blanche lives in one of the houses at the closed off end of the Close and Jeremy and Sandy's family live opposite. A large, sloping, front lawn runs down from their front path to the front path belonging to Blanche and her family. All the front gardens in Overwood Close are supposed to be open plan, but a row of tall, clipped conifer trees makes a sort of tall, boundary hedge between these two homes.

However, the cats living in the vicinity of Overwood Close do not recognise this boundary, or boundaries of any kind. They feel very strongly about the subject and some time ago they decided to form the Cats Association Against Land Enclosure (CAALE). The association has a clear anti-boundary policy and all members have the fundamental right to roam freely in and out of all the gardens in the area. But this does not apply to houses. Houses are different as the individual cat owners have complete control over them. Visitors can only go inside if the cat owner invites them to do so. Policies such as these have ensured that the association has become a popular and influential organisation. Indeed, it has become so popular and powerful that a unanimous decision has been taken to ensure that it continues to flourish. Some time ago, membership was made compulsory for all the kittens born to existing members.

When the CAALE was first formed, it was obvious that Blanche would be voted in as the first Chaircat. Everyone agreed that she would be a safe pair of paws and this has proved to be the case. She has consistently shown that she is intelligent, brave and fair. These were the very qualities that were needed in a leader because the Chaircat would be responsible for many duties and responsibilities. Blanche has proved more than equal to the task and is held in the highest regard by all her members.

CHAPTER 1

Back Shed

There he is again, the third morning in a row. Swanning around as if he owns the place. Tail swishing, smiling his smug smile and nodding his head condescendingly at the other cats. He thinks he looks so cool. What he doesn't realise is that when he nods like that it draws attention to his double chin.

The sight of him makes Blanche want to spit. He knows he has no right or reason to be here, it's not his manor. This is CAALE (Cats Association Against Land Enclosure) territory and smarmy Back Shed knows it. Oh yes! He knows about the association's rules because she can't count the number of times he has tried to join and been knocked back. But he just can't get it through his thick head that he's not wanted. He's crude, rude and so full of himself; not the sort of cat Blanche wants hanging around.

Apart from anything else, he doesn't even live in Overwood Close, or in any of the other addresses the association covers. Blanche has it on very good authority that he lives some distance away, in one of those big town houses in the middle of Wells. The ones with the long windows and the long back gardens and that's where he should stay.

Blanche has had a go at him about trespassing on association land over and over again. And every time he has tried to join the CAALE, she has done her best to put her intense dislike of him aside. She has patiently explained that, as the Chaircat of the association, she has to make sure that all membership applicants have to go through certain procedures before they can be considered as suitable members. They have to attend an induction session and then have an interview. She has also pointed out that, even if he did well at the induction session and interview, she has to make her recommendations to the association committee and she couldn't recommend him because he doesn't meet the criteria to qualify for membership. She has told him over and over again that to qualify, cats have to live in the right catchment area.

She has even threatened him with an official warning if he doesn't stop hanging around the Close but it goes in one ear and out the other. It's quite obvious that he does not respect her or the office of Chaircat. He just smiles annoyingly and stabs a plump paw in her face and yells. 'I'm not going through a stupid interview and you can't stop me coming into your Close because The Great God of Cat Territory sent me a sign. The sign said that I am a chosen, travelling cat and I have the right to find a place to eat and sleep wherever I want to. I am not tied to one place to live. *So*, you can't stop me coming here because The Great God of Cat Territory is more important that the Chaircat of the CAALE.'

Blanche knew he was lying his head off. Nobody had heard of The Great God of Cat Territory. As if that wasn't enough, he kids himself that no one has heard about his comfortable, home down in the middle of Wells; he acts as if it is a closely guarded secret. He puts on a big act about not having a permanent address. According to him, he is a special cat. He isn't ordinary like the other cats. He tries to convince anyone who will listen that he gave up the security and easy life of a loving household years ago. Instead, he chose to see the world and has survived against all the odds. In his head, he is a cat legend.

He never stops trying to give the impression that he is a brave, free spirit, a free spirit who is not tied to anything or anyone. Playing the part of a wise, world-weary wanderer, he often sits in the middle of the Close singing the lines from an old song called, 'Wherever I Lay My Hat, That's My Home'. The older cats sniff and pay no attention to his stupid song. They know he is settled in one of the plushest households in Wells and they also know that he doesn't have a hat either. However, the younger ones are easily impressed and often join in with the song. Back Shed calls them his 'Little Groupies'.

He likes having a fan club, it feeds his already inflated ego. Completely ignoring the way the older cats resent him, he acts like a puffed-up, feline Pied Piper. Gathering the younger cats around him he tells them stories of danger and adventure. Their eyes grow wider and wider as each of his tales become more and more fantastic. He then launches into the story of his life. They have listened to the story of his life many, many times and don't seem to mind that he has a habit of repeating himself. Some of them can even mouth most of it along with him because it's nearly always the same. In a serious voice he leans forward, beginning with the words, 'Now listen carefully, when I was your age I lived on a ship that took people from one place to another.'

Hearing the story for the first time, two or three little cats had raised their paws in the air, shouting, 'What's a ship, what's a ship?'

Finding a stick, Back Shed had drawn a picture of a ship in the dry earth underneath the line of conifers separating Blanche's garden from the garden belonging to Jeremy and Sandy. 'Now, this is a ship and a ship sails on the ocean and the ocean is the biggest pond ever.' He had added a few wavy, water lines under the ship. 'The ocean is also called The Big Sea of Wee because that is where all the wee, that people do, is sent. When it is windy, huge rolls of wee water blow up and they can break a ship and knock people and cats into the rough water. When they are in the water, they sink down and down and until they can't sink anymore, nobody knows what happens to them after that.'

The little cats had loved the drawing of a ship and insisted that Back Shed should do one each time he told his tale. He was only too pleased to oblige and now he even encourages some of them to try and do drawings of their own. When the drawing class is over, they crouch down in a semi-circle while he tells them about the days when he was old enough to sail in ships around a faraway place called the Greek Islands. His best friend, a large tabby cat called John, always sailed with him. They were very close and had been together for a long, long time.

One terrible day, John was knocked into the ocean by the most gigantic roll of wee water ever. As he sank down, Back Shed tried to save him but the rolls of wee water were breaking the ship and he fell into the ocean himself. He managed to stop sinking down by frantically paddling his paws, but he couldn't see John anywhere. His heart felt as if it was breaking as he realised that it was too late. When Back Shed reaches this point in the story his voice always becomes shaky and tears fill his eyes. 'My friend, my best friend was gone forever.' Hanging his head, he whispers, 'I should have saved him.'

His fan club know that this is the part of the story where he expects them to cry. Cuddling each other, they sob and sing the special song that Back Shed has taught them (they sing it to the tune of 'Oh Where, Oh Where has my Little Dog Gone?'):

♪ *Poor John, poor John, oh where have you gone?*
Down, down, down in the sea,
Poor John, poor John, oh where have you gone?
Try not to drink any wee. ♪

When the song is finished, Back Shed wipes his eyes and explains that he was only saved himself because he managed to scramble onto a piece of wood from the broken ship and was picked up by a passing fishing boat days later. 'My life was changed forever, my young friends. I made up my mind that I would never sail on the ocean again. I would travel the land alone.'

The rest of his life story usually tends to trail off at this point and becomes a bit disjointed. The youngest cats always have a problem staying awake as he drones on. They try to look as if they are still listening, but it's a bit tricky because Back Shed's voice always lapses into a droning babble, getting faster and higher. It ends up sounding like the persistent buzz, buzz, buzzing of an insect on a summer's day and sometimes it sends them into a deep sleep.

Blanche wonders how much longer he can carry on telling

his old stories. If he actually did have any adventures, they were a long time ago. These days, he enjoys the easy life. It is true that, when he arrived in Wells, he was homeless but he was only homeless for a very short time.

He spent his first night in a shed at the bottom of a long, walled garden. The posh people who owned the garden spotted him the next morning and couldn't wait to adopt him. Of course, he played up to them, making out that he was lost and lonely. What a poser! But it worked and all they wanted to do was to spoil their new pet. They couldn't wait to rush out to buy the softest cat duvet and the best cat food they could find. Of course it wasn't long before the signs of his cosseted life started to show and he began to put on quite a bit of weight.

The fact that he is now getting pudgier by the day hasn't dented his ego though. He chooses not to notice his chubby stomach and bottom. He just strolls around as if he's the most handsome cat in Somerset. Sometimes, he even has the nerve to playfully sway his bottom from side to side when he walks. Blanche calls him 'wobbly cheeks' and tells him that his bum swaying makes him look ridiculous. But nothing she says, or does, seems to have any effect on the totally misguided view that Back Shed has of himself. As far as he is concerned, he is a star, a celebrity, an idol. He is still the dashing, romantic hero of his swashbuckling stories.

But there is one thing that does get to him. The one thing that does drive him insane with anger is his name. He won't accept the fact that it is his own fault that he is called Back Shed. Yet, ironically, he did actually bring it on himself. When he visited the Close for the first time, he wouldn't tell anyone his real name because he wanted to create an air of mystery. But his plan backfired massively because a few of the resident cats thought he was trying to hide his identity. Perhaps he had a terrible secret he had to conceal? They rushed to tell Blanche and when she heard this piece of news, she called an emergency meeting of the CAALE immediately.

The cats were always careful not to give their people any reason to suspect that they held meetings, so they often agreed to gather in Blanche's garage. They always made sure that the white, metal, pull-down door was half-closed making it difficult for anyone passing to see the group of cats inside. Blanche opened the meeting. 'We can't have a cat coming into the Close without a name. As your Chaircat, I need to know such important information.' The cats all nodded. Blanche went on and pointed at The Wise White Cat, the most revered cat in the association, 'I think we should ask The Wise White Cat what he thinks we should do.' Again, the cats all nodded.

The Wise White Cat took a deep breath and slowly stretched out on the floor and folded his front paws. 'Every cat should have a name, but this cat will not tell us his name. He has told us that it was a dark night when he came to Wells. He has told us that he was lost and had nowhere to sleep. He has told us that he found a shed in the back garden of a posh house in Wells and he slept there.' Pausing, The Wise White Cat held up a paw, then closing his eyes, he announced, 'I say that he shall be called Back Shed from this day until he is taken by The Great Cat God of Forever Sleep.' Blanche thought this was a terrific name and patted The Wise White cat on the back. When the other cats saw that Blanche liked the name, they all said they liked it too.

'Great name, good name, it suits him,' they chimed together.

When he found out what he was going to be called, Back Shed was furious. 'No, no, no,' he shouted, 'you can't call me that, I am a free cat, I am a lone travelling cat, I do not belong to anyone, I should have a name that suits the cat I am. I want a formal inquiry so I can lodge a protest.' But it was too late; he had broken CAALE custom by refusing to take any notice of Blanche when she warned him that he was trespassing on association land. That meant that he couldn't claim any association rights at all. More importantly, The Wise White Cat had given him his name and that meant that it couldn't be changed under any circumstances. Everyone deferred to The Wise White Cat's word because The Wise White Cat's word was The Wise White Cat's word.

It served him right. It's not as if every single one of the older cats haven't realised that all his talk about being a dare devil, free cat was rubbish. It sticks out a mile that he loves being looked after by the people in the posh house. His long, black fur is sleek and shiny; sometimes his people even try to weave the longer fur between his ears into two little plaits. But Back Shed still refuses to see that he has become one of the most petted cats in Wells. He just carries on telling his stories of adventure and pretending he knows more about life and the wide world, than anyone else.

CHAPTER 2

Sussout University

When he spots Blanche, sitting by her open window, Back Shed yells, 'Yo!' and punches the air with a fat, furry front paw. He obviously thinks this gesture gives him the kind of 'street credibility' he craves, but Blanche ignores him. She will put him in his place later. At the moment, she has other things on her mind and they demand all her attention.

The early morning is fine and the front lawn is waiting to be bathed in the gift of early sunlight. Blanche loves days like this. She loves the delicious smells of late summer. They drift into the house along with the shafts of thermal gold sent from above by The Great Cat God of Light and Warmth. However, the sight of Back Shed has set her teeth on edge and has spoiled the moment.

As usual, she is sitting on the low, long, white PVC windowsill in the living room at the front of her house. From her windowsill she can see everything that is happening in Overwood Close.

Of course, she has ultimate responsibility for the security of all association land but she monitors Overwood Close personally. Normally, she enjoys this duty and feels relaxed when she is checking the identities and movements of all those who come and go. More often than not, she smiles and waves graciously at the familiar faces, reassuring them that all is well and there is nothing to worry about.

Although the Close is small and secluded, she makes this daily check her first duty of the day. But as the Chaircat of the CAALE she has to make sure that everyone else living in CAALE territory is also kept safe and secure. She relies on the cats living in nearby roads and lanes for all their latest information about the comings and goings of any strangers they may spot. If an unknown cat suddenly appears anywhere in her area and it looks like he or she is going to settle in a nearby house, the association's spy network kicks in. The newcomer is secretly watched day and night and Blanche receives regular updates on their general behaviour and habits. Blanche pays attention to all the updates and always makes sure that nothing is overlooked. As a rule, she couldn't be more conscientious about security.

But not today, today Blanche is restless and she is not even doing a proper security check of Overwood Close. Instead of reassuringly waving her paw at everyone, she has stuffed it into her mouth and is chewing and biting her claws. She just can't take pleasure in her work or the glorious, quiet morning and she has to admit that it isn't all Back Shed's fault. She was in an odd mood even before she saw him. In fact, her thoughts have been all jumbled ever since she woke up and she hasn't been able to get her head straight, no matter how hard she tries. Her instincts seem to be warning her that all is not as it should be. She feels change in the air. The kind of change that will plunge her home and family into a state of unimaginable chaos. The same feelings keep lurching through her body and clouding her thoughts.

Eventually, she manages to work out that it all started days ago. She had been sitting next to Lucy on the sofa when her ears had pricked up. Lucy was talking to one of her friends on the phone. She was going on and on and on about going away to an unknown place called Sussout University.

'Yeah, it will be so cool, I can't wait. Yeah, my dad's driving me up there. My mum wants to come but there won't be room in the car. I've got so much stuff, you wouldn't believe. I think it takes about four or five hours to get there. Yeah, we'll have a real blast when you come to visit me. You can meet all my new friends. What do you mean, if I have any?' Laughing, Lucy had ended the call,

What she had heard didn't actually worry Blanche all that much at the time. She had often listened to Lucy talking to her friends and making plans. No, it wasn't that call alone. It was that call, plus what she had heard later that day that had first set the alarm bells ringing. She was staring at a spider running over the lounge carpet, when the raised voices of Clare and Andrew, Lucy's parents, broke her concentration. They were in the kitchen, having a heated conversation about Lucy leaving home and living in halls (whatever that meant). Clare didn't sound too happy. 'Of course I'm proud of her, of course I want her to get a degree but she's going such a long way away. What if she falls in with the wrong crowd? Especially in her first year when she is living on campus, she probably won't eat properly or get enough sleep either.'

Sounding on edge himself, Andrew had told her to stop putting a damper on everything. 'She will be fine, she won't do anything stupid. Why do you have to keep harping on about all the things that could go wrong and student debt and the importance of regular hot meals and vitamin pills? Don't you want her to go? Don't you trust her?' he demanded.

Almost in tears Clare had nodded her head. 'Of course I do, of course I do but I can't help worrying, she's our only child for heaven's sake.'

'Look, we want her to get a decent job, don't we? How is she going to do that without a degree?'

Clare had shrugged her shoulders. 'Getting a degree doesn't always mean you get a good job these days.' With that, she pulled her sagging tracksuit bottoms up so far that they almost reached her chest and stalked off to the spare room to stare at the growing mountain of packing. Blanche followed her, she had been wondering about the mountain for some time and had kept checking it out as it got bigger and bigger. So far, it included a couple of saucepans, towels, pillows, sheets, a duvet and a new black and white Ikea duvet cover, a big red bean bag, some cutlery, a mug with a skull on it and three posters.

With a jolt, Blanche remembered that this was the point when she had started to have a sense of foreboding. After listening to Clare and Andrew arguing about Lucy going away, she realised that Lucy was going to take the mountain with her when she went. But working that out hadn't really helped because it didn't explain why or where or when she was going.

This was the problem, everything was up in the air and the uncertainty was really getting to her. This was why she was having such disturbing feelings.

Slowly shaking her head from side to side, she asked herself how was she supposed to get to grips with everything she was seeing and hearing? For a start, she didn't know anything about Sussout University; she didn't even know how long they would be away. Of course, Lucy had gone away for short periods before, but this time it was different.

Lucy was obviously leaving for a long, long time, which made Blanche absolutely certain that she must be going with her.

Ever since Blanche's kitten days it had been understood that she and Lucy were pledged to one another for life. According to The Cat Code of Loyalty, such a pledge was impossible to break. Where Lucy went, Blanche must follow. Of course, her life and obligations to the CAALE were important, but her love and loyalty to Lucy were non- negotiable. Blanche gave a little groan as she realised that she could soon be called upon to perform the ultimate act of self-sacrifice and abandon her home, her family and her friends in order to fulfil that pledge.

She knew all about the theory that travel was a good way to broaden the mind, but she could not agree. Like most of the other cats she knew, she believed that a cat should stay on home ground. After all, your home and family make you what you are. But, it looked as if her own thoughts and beliefs about travel would have to be put to one side. If Lucy was going to be moving away from the Close, then she would have to move too.

Staring blindly out of the window, cold shivers ran up and down her back as she became more and more agitated. If only she could understand what was happening but nobody was bothering to involve her and she was beginning to get desperate. She needed to get some answers, but how?

Strictly speaking, she should be talking to The Wise White

Cat. He was very understanding and everyone went to him when they were worried or stressed. He only lived next door and he was always ready to listen. But Blanche didn't want to discuss her problem with him yet. What could she tell him? She only had feelings and unconfirmed suspicions so she would probably only end up sounding neurotic. Before she talked to him, she needed to find out more facts and details if she could. The one cat who might know something was Little Treasure, her birth daughter. After all, Little Treasure shared the same house and might have heard something. But asking her was a risky business because nobody ever asked her about anything. What was the point? Little Treasure had the brain-power of an intellectually challenged flea. Blanche was only too aware that her own reputation could be permanently damaged if the other cats in the association thought she was taking advice from her scatterbrained daughter. If word got out that Blanche had done anything so reckless, there was a chance that the members may lose all the respect they had for her. They might even begin to wonder if she was still suitable to be the Chaircat of the CAALE.

CHAPTER 3

Little Treasure

Most Siamese cats are attractive, sleek and graceful but it has to be said that Blanche is touch disappointing in the looks department. She does have the distinctive colouring of a seal point Siamese cat but not the usual body shape. She is not exactly overweight, just a little on the stocky side and a bit clumsy. Some of the cats in the Close have also noticed that a few of her personal habits can be a bit off-putting. But when Little Treasure was born, it soon became obvious to everyone that Blanche had given birth to a perfect example of the breed.

Little Treasure is exquisite; her stunning good looks take your breath away. Her cream coloured fur is ravishing and shines like the finest silk. The dark brown markings on her fine-boned face set off her sparkling, sapphire-blue eyes perfectly. Cats and people would sigh with pleasure when they saw her for the first time. 'She is so lovely,' they would murmur. As they watched her growing more beautiful every day, everyone agreed that she was becoming a real little treasure.

'We will have to think of a name for her soon, she is nearly seven weeks old,' Clare had sighed when the family were sitting together at the dining table after their Sunday lunch.

'I think that I already have,' Lucy replied with a knowing twinkle in her eyes. 'Listen to what people are saying. They are calling her a little treasure and that should be her name. In fact, I have decided that it is peachy-perfect. From this day on, Blanche's kitten will be known as Little Treasure.'

Andrew's mouth fell open in disbelief. He was drinking a mug of coffee at the time and he ended up dribbling most of it down the front of his T-shirt. 'Are you insane? Have you thought about calling her to come into the house at night to be brushed? Even worse, what about when we want her to come indoors during the day when there are more people about? What are they going to think when I'm yelling, "Little Treasure, Little Treasure?" I'll sound like a real weirdo. It's a totally ridiculous name.' Leaping up in exasperation, he charged off to change his T-shirt.

Watching him flouncing through the kitchen on his way upstairs, Lucy gave a drawn-out, 'Oooooo!' and shifted her gaze to the newly named Little Treasure. She was rolling around, playing with the fringe on the rug. Kneeling down Lucy cuddled her and turned to Clare, 'Look, look she loves it too, I know she thinks I have made exactly the right choice, haven't I sweetie?' she crooned into her ear. 'After all, I was the one who decided to call your mother Blanche so I have a proven track record with naming cats. Clare wasn't convinced but she was sure she saw the kitten flutter her eyelids and smile happily.

At first, the reaction to the name was not exactly encouraging. Most of the cats laughed behind their paws when they heard it. But as time passed, they had to admit that it did suit her because she was becoming prettier and prettier every day. However, it seemed that a pretty cat is one thing and an intelligent cat is another. Strictly speaking, Little Treasure should have been born with the ability to learn all the necessary cat skills she needs to get on in life; her beauty should just be a bonus. But everyone in the Close soon realised that Little Treasure was not developing normal cat know-how. In other words, as she began to grow up, it became clear that she was not going to follow the chosen way to cat maturity. And she was definitely not going to take after Blanche in the brains department. All the signs were pointing to the fact that she was turning into an exception to the rule.

Sadly, the problem wasn't spotted by her mother until it was too late. Blanche was so busy with her work for the CAALE that she hadn't realised that Little Treasure was not turning out the way that she should be. Blanche hadn't appreciated how damaging all the admiring attention was to an impressionable, adolescent female like Little Treasure. Instead of learning the normal cat skills, she has become addicted to the lavish compliments that have been heaped upon her day after day. Things have now reached the stage where her vanity has taken over her life and she is only interested in thinking and talking about the way she looks.

Blanche knows that the time will come when she will have to take a firm paw. She will have to face up to the fact that Little Treasure has lost all sense of cat reality. It's obvious that she isn't the least bit interested in routine cat issues and is obsessed with how to make herself look more and more gorgeous every minute of every day. She spends hours smoothing her fur in front of the full-length mirror in the bathroom and using Lucy's hair mascara to touch up her eyebrows. When she doesn't look perfect, she stamps her paws on the floor and wails, 'I'm a beauty icon, I can't go out looking like this.'

Blanche wonders where it will all end. She hopes that Clare doesn't leave any magazines, with pictures of the benefits of cosmetic surgery lying around. Little Treasure might start to get bizarre ideas about having a face-lift or a tummy-tuck when she gets older. The way she is going, it could happen.

As a rule, Blanche would prefer to throw herself into the garden pond than try to get any sense out of the one cat who didn't have any. But that was the whole point, things were not normal. She sighed and with a heavy heart jumped down from the windowsill and reluctantly walked through the lounge to find her.

Little Treasure was not far away; Blanche just had to go through the open, sliding, glass doors, which screened the lounge from the dining area at the back of the house. She was stretched out on a sunny patch of carpet in front of the open patio doors, which lead from the dining area into the small back garden.

From the patio doors, two steps lead down to the rectangular lawn, which takes up most of the compact garden. Andrew cuts the grass regularly and trims the sweet-smelling shrubs and roses in the borders. There is a small greenhouse to the right and a rockery, with a pond, to the left. In the middle of the pond, a tiny fountain tinkles onto water-lily leaves.

But the best thing about the garden is the view. If you stand at the top of the two steps, it's possible to see over roofs, church steeples and the Cathedral towers of Wells Cathedral as far as the mystical Glastonbury Tor.

Feeling a pang in her heart, Blanche lifted her head to look beyond Little Treasure, out over the sunlit garden toward Glastonbury. This place meant so much to her and she wasn't sure how she would cope when she had to leave it behind.

Little Treasure wasn't interested in the view; she was enjoying the sunshine while she worked on her beauty routine. The rays of the sun, which streamed in through the patio doors, lit up her silken fur and made it shine like the purest, polished silver. She was busily buffing and shaping the claws on her left front paw with a small, pink emery board. Blanche hesitated when she saw what Little Treasure was doing. She became even more convinced that asking her to discuss anything, except the way she looked, would turn out to be a complete waste of time. But she was desperate and desperation often causes intelligent cats to do strange things.

Trying to keep things low-key, Blanche smiled at Little Treasure. 'Have you heard all this talk about my Lucy going off somewhere?' Tilting her head to one side she waited, but nothing came back from her daughter. Little Treasure was playing for time, she did not respond well to leading questions. She thought that the cats who asked them were just trying to make her look stupid. She decided to pretend she had not heard Blanche. Concentrating very hard, she put down her emery board and started to polish her claws with a little piece of pale, blue velvet. With a self-satisfied smirk, she remembered how she had discovered it sewn into the patchwork bedspread in the spare bedroom.

Dozing on the spare bed one afternoon, she noticed that the velvet patch felt soft to the touch. Rubbing it against her cheek, she caught her reflection in the dressing table mirror. Realising that the colour brought out the beautiful blue of her eyes, and made them sparkle even more, she sighed with pleasure. 'It's so me, I look fabulous.' Excitedly, she decided, there and then, that she just had to have it. Gradually she had loosened the stitches, which secured it to the quilt with her beautifully shaped sharp, little, teeth. Eventually, she managed to pull it free and took possession of it in triumph.

Ever since then, Little Treasure kept her prize with her whenever she was in the house and she had become very possessive about it. She found that she could use it for lots of beauty treatments, including toning up her face fur as well as polishing her claws.

When Blanche had noticed how often she kept stroking it, she saw it as another sign that Little Treasure was becoming seriously unbalanced. 'Have you ever had a think about why you want possessions like your piece of blue velvet? Do you really need it?'

'Yes, I do need it and no, I have never had a think about why I want it, I don't have to. Only people go on about why they want things. Cats just have to know that they want something, not why they want it or if they need it. Anyway, you never think about why you want to roll around on Jeremy and Sandy's hall carpet all the time, do you?'

Surprisingly, Little Treasure's answer stopped Blanche in her tracks. Maybe she had a point. But the last thing that Blanche wanted was the piece of velvet issue leading to a discussion about her own behaviour so she hadn't brought up the subject again. Even if she had, Little Treasure would probably have stamped her paws and become huffy. It was more than likely she would have accused Blanche of trying to persuade her to get rid of her piece of velvet so that she could secretly retrieve it later and keep it for herself.

Little Treasure continued to ignore Blanche. However, it was obvious from her rapid eye movements that she had heard what she had said about Lucy going away. Although she tried to look unconcerned, it was easy to see that she was nervous. She clutched her piece of velvet tightly in her paw and started to hum a snatch of music from the Bollywood film she had watched the day before.

Bollywood films were Little Treasure's only other burning passion. She had been a big fan long before they had become so popular. She first saw one on television ages ago and was instantly hooked. Lucy had left the TV on one morning and, with nothing better to do, Little Treasure sat down to watch it. A Bollywood film started and suddenly the lounge was filled with the happiest music she had ever heard; she could hardly believe her ears. When the dancing started she was thrilled and couldn't help trying to join in.

Of course, she did not know how to move to the music or do the charming hand movements then, but things had changed since those early days. Now, she was good. She could follow the dance routines with poise and precision. She could also sing along with the Bollywood music, copying the Bollywood stars. Her naturally high-pitched voice blended in perfectly with the way the singers delivered their songs.

Singing loudly, she would dance around the lounge until she felt dizzy. Arching her eyebrows and using her eyes flirtatiously, she would toss her head at the cat or cats who happened to be visiting the garden at the time. Mesmerised, they would gape at her, open-mouthed, through the glass of the patio doors. Little Treasure was convinced that they were awe-struck with admiration and envy. Spurred on by this thought, she had made up her mind to find a way to impress them even more with her musical talent and beauty.

Lately, she had begun to form a plan to get hold of the, long, red and gold tassels on the silk cushion in Clare and Andy's bedroom. She might be able to chew them off the way she had chewed off her piece of blue velvet. Then, if she could work out a way of fixing a couple of the tassels to her head or her ears, she would look fantastic, just like a Bollywood heroine in a Bollywood blockbuster. Perhaps more cats would turn up to watch her singing and dancing. Who knows, she may even become famous as the most beautiful and talented cat in the area? Fantasies of crowds of cats waving their paws in the air and chanting her name floated through her mind. She would give ecstatic sighs as she bowed and blew kisses to her imaginary audience.

Blanche began to get fed up with Little Treasure's humming and decided to try again. 'Do you think Lucy is getting ready to go off somewhere?' Once again, Little Treasure did not respond and carried on humming. Blanche, already stressed out over the Lucy situation, felt her patience running out. Her smile slipped and she clenched her jaws, hissing, 'If you don't answer me, I'll tie you up and give you a cheap home perm. It will make you look like a demented poodle. Everyone will laugh at you and you won't be able to do anything about it for weeks.'

This terrifying prospect electrified Little Treasure and she snapped out of her Bollywood humming act. Blinking nervously and delicately wiping her brow with her blue velvet she said quickly, 'I haven't noticed anything that points to your Lucy going anywhere.' She added thoughtfully, 'Your age has a lot to do with the way you are reacting to things at the moment you know, it's to be expected.' Then she threw herself into an elegant head over heels on the carpet and whispered something about hormones and emotions.

'Brilliant,' Blanche muttered to herself, 'very helpful.' Little Treasure had obviously been watching those women's programmes on television again. Why couldn't she just stick to her Bollywood films?

Her useless conversation with Little Treasure left Blanche feeling fed up and frustrated. She knew that she shouldn't have bothered. Slowly walking back through the living room, she returned to her position on the windowsill. She sat there for some time, moodily staring out at nothing in particular. Despite the fact that Little Treasure appeared to be in the dark about what was going on, Blanche's cat instinct kept telling her that

BOLLYWOOD

something traumatic was about to happen and it definitely had something to do with Lucy going away. All that university stuff that Clare and Andrew were always talking about these days was a sure sign that something was up. Answers, answers, answers, she just had to get some answers from someone or somewhere.

CHAPTER 4

Jeremy and Sandy

While Blanche was turning things over in her mind, she caught sight of Jeremy and Sandy, the cats from the house opposite. They were sitting outside their front door, also enjoying the gift of morning sunlight. Jeremy was sitting on one side of the door and Sandy was sitting on the other. Blanche watched them for a while. She was pleased to see that there was no sign of Back Shed. With a bit of luck, the fool had gone home.

Jeremy and Sandy had lived together in the same house for years, but they both liked their own space. They did not feel the need to be joined at the hip and often chose to go their own way. However, this did not stop Jeremy from following Sandy around when he wanted to know what he was up to.

Still feeling a bit deflated after wasting her time trying to get information out of Little Treasure, Blanche decided to talk things over with them. Who knows, they may be able to help? It was worth a try anyway. She scrambled down through the open window and landed, with a thump, on the lawn below. She plodded across the sweep of grass, through the hedge of tall conifers, toward their front door.

As they saw her approaching, both Jeremy and Sandy gave Blanche a respectful nod.

Sandy is younger than Jeremy, but he is bigger. In fact, he is massive. He has a huge round head and huge round paws. But nature has played a cruel trick on Sandy. Everyone agrees that he is impressive to look at. His ginger and white fur is immaculate and his beautiful, hazel eyes shine with health and good humour. But the way he sounds doesn't match the way he looks. He has a very high-pitched voice and sometimes, it is difficult to keep a straight face when Sandy is speaking.

Jeremy is the worst offender and often sniggers when Sandy starts to say something.

This must be difficult for Sandy, but he always pretends not to notice when Jeremy starts making fun of him. Although Sandy is a strong, male cat, he does not like getting involved in hurtful bickering. He tries to avoid saying or doing anything that might lead to a row or a fight because he is caring and sensitive. But the real reason he doesn't lose his temper and have a go at Jeremy is because he is pretty certain that Jeremy can't help the way he behaves.

Like Little Treasure, Jeremy has issues about his appearance and Sandy has watched him brooding about it for hours on end. But Jeremy isn't exactly like Little Treasure; he isn't obsessively vain. Quite the opposite, he can't bear to see himself in a mirror because he is tormented by the way he looks. He hates the fact that he isn't like the other cats. Sandy is fairly sure that this is why Jeremy pokes fun at the physical shortcomings of others. Somehow, it's the only way he knows how to make himself feel better about himself.

Sandy has accepted that Jeremy's behaviour has made sharing a house with him difficult at times. It's not just that he laughs at him when he speaks. The other thing is that he is a worrier. When he isn't tormenting himself over the way he looks, he always manages to find something else to fret about. But, it's blindingly obvious that it is his appearance that is his major hang-up. The thing is, Sandy can't work out how to help.

The other cats in the Close agree with Sandy. They can't understand why Jeremy goes on the way he does and why he has to spend most of his time in such a state. They think that he should try to get over himself because he is really quite handsome. He is not too fat or too thin and he has attractive black and white markings. On the rare occasion, when he does manage to relax and enjoy himself, he even has an appealing, bashful smile.

It is true that there is something different about him, but he's not all that different. He only has an extra toe on each of his front paws, but the problem is, he can't come up with a reason why he was born that way. Why didn't The Great God of Cat Creation make him in the same way as He made all other cats? Jeremy thinks it may be because he was never supposed to be a proper cat. Perhaps The Great God of Cat Creation just made him for a joke? Jeremy can't get these thoughts out of his head and is terrified that, if he doesn't hide his front paws whenever he can, the other cats will start to reject him. They may refuse to speak to him and he might even be thrown out of the CAALE.

To try and turn his problem into something positive he has told a few of the local cats that his extra toes have been passed down from a royal ancestor. He told them that he is descended from Anne Boleyn. Of course, nobody believed him and laughed in his face. Then he tried to win them round by getting their sympathy. He told them that Anne Boleyn was persecuted and had her head cut off because she had the same deformity as he did.

It is true that Anne Boleyn, the second wife of Henry VIII, was supposed to have one extra finger on her hand. It is also true that she was actually beheaded in the year of 1536. But Jeremy's explanation of her death didn't fool anyone. The local cats knew a bit about Anne Boleyn because they all know about the Tudor period.

When the Tudors were on the throne (and for some time before and after), people blamed cats for all sorts of things. They were accused of helping witches to put spells on people and innocent cats were tortured and killed. This period is the most well known in cat history because it was a cruel age for their ancestors and stories about it have been passed on to each generation; they call it the 'Dark Time'.

Blanche wished that Jeremy would stop banging on about the 'Dark Time' and Anne Boleyn. It made the little ones cry and the grown-up cats complained. In her capacity as Chaircat of the CAALE, Blanche was definitely going to have it out with him when she had worked out what to say. She had to be careful to handle it in the right way though because he actually seemed to be going off his head lately. His attempts to make his extra toes more acceptable and interesting were becoming more and more ludicrous and he had begun to talk about being beheaded like Anne Boleyn if too many cats or people found out about his extra toes.

As a protective measure, Jeremy had developed a way of moving and squatting because he thought it hid his flawed paws. But it did not really work when he was squatting, as he never managed to spread his weight evenly, often toppling over when he lost his balance. Of course, this meant that he ended up showing the very paws he was trying to hide. Everyone who knew about his fear of being rejected, or beheaded, tried to reassure Jeremy that he did not have to cover up his paws. He was not in any danger if they became exposed. They argued that he was safe because cutting off heads was not legal in the United Kingdom any more.

Even The Wise White Cat had a word and advised him to overcome his extra toe phobia. Taking him to one side after a CAALE meeting, he put his paw on Jeremy's head, saying, 'Outward features are not important, do not hide or feel ashamed of physical features. It is the cat within that matters.'

With a forced smile, Jeremy just nodded and wandered off disrespectfully muttering, 'What do you know?'

Blanche had been hanging about after that meeting and watched as Jeremy walked away from The Wise White Cat with his head hanging down. He looked very dejected. She decided to step in and follow him. As the Chaircat of the CAALE, Blanche knew she shouldn't be caught out telling lies. But she told herself that sometimes little lies were necessary.

Catching up with him, and trying to look knowledgeable, she whispered in his ear, 'Anne Boleyn lost her head because she was no good at catching mice, it had nothing to do with her extra finger.' But Jeremy obviously did not believe her, even if she was the Chaircat of the CAALE. He just carried on muttering to himself and flicking his tail from side to side. Shrugging her shoulders, Blanche realised that she couldn't get through to him so she had left the subject alone for the time being.

She certainly wasn't going to bring it up today. She was adamant that was not going to let Jeremy turn her problems into an opportunity to talk about his issues. She was going to stick to her guns and avoid being drawn into his extra toe problem no matter what he said or did. Surely, he would sense that she had more pressing matters on her mind. Not only was she becoming frantic about the Sussout University thing but she also had to deal with Back Shed and have a talk with Little Treasure and Jeremy about their obsessive behaviour.

Stopping to sniff the grass and admire the daisies, she wished she could just forget everything and enjoy the beautiful morning instead of feeling so agitated about her own and Lucy's future. The earth smelled wonderful and the daisies made her smile. She longed to forget her responsibilities, worries and confusion. She longed to skip around the front lawn in a wild celebration of the beauties of nature, but the time and place were not right.

Of course, skipping around would be acceptable at any time if she had just done a good poo. Cat protocol decrees that, after a good poo, cats can gambol up and down front lawns as often as they like without attracting any disapproval. In fact, they can gambol almost anywhere, including the inside of their own houses. Everyone knows that when you have finished pooing, there is nothing better than skipping around on the grass or rushing inside your house then rushing outside over and over again. A good poo does that to cats. But Blanche had not just done a good poo so there was no excuse for skipping. Skipping without the poo factor was a bit risky; it would not go down well with the cat community.

Apart from anything else, she knew that such an inappropriate, public display could destroy all the respect and credibility that she had so carefully built up. She had always been very conscious of her image as Chaircat of the CAALE and took care to leave her more bouncy behaviour for the privacy of the back garden. With another sigh she went to join Sandy and Jeremy to try and find out if they had any ideas about what was going on.

Blanche found it difficult to put her worries into words. After all, as Chaircat of the CAALE, she was supposed to be knowledgeable, sensible and calm in a crisis. Yet here she was with a problem she could not fully explain and could not solve. She took a deep breath and plunged in. But as she started to tell them about her doubts and anxieties, she became distracted. Despite her determination to stay focused, she couldn't help noticing that Jeremy had started to topple from his typical, precarious, sitting position onto his left side.

As usual, he was trying to hide his front paws from view and as usual, he had tucked them too far under his stomach as he crouched down. Of course, this made it difficult for him to keep his balance. As he started to tip over to the left he attempted one of his bashful smiles. Mistakenly, he thought that if he kept smiling Blanche and Sandy may not realise what was going on. His smile got wider and wider as he tried harder and harder to look as if everything was okay but his mind was working overtime. How could he set himself straight before he made a complete fool of himself? Frantically, he tried to stop the toppling before he rolled down the sloping front path. But things were slipping out of control; he really was losing his balance and starting to panic. His smile became desperate and he actually ended up looking a bit scary.

But Jeremy should have had more faith in his friends because both Blanche and Sandy worked out what was happening at the same time. They quickly sprang into action and levered his left side upward so that he was in a crouching position again. He was still a bit lopsided, but at least he looked fairly stable and his front paws were still well hidden. Sandy trilled out a high-pitched giggle of relief and Blanche gave a soft grunt of satisfaction as she patted the fur on Jeremy's left shoulder back into place. She did not say anything about what had just occurred because she knew what would happen.

Jeremy would either start banging on about his extra toes or become overwhelmed with embarrassment. Then her worst fears would be realised; the conversation would be hijacked. So, ignoring the episode, she settled down and made a second attempt to tell them what was bothering her.

She drew in her breath and said in a low voice, 'I know there are big changes happening at our place.' Then she added, 'But, I am not sure why.'

She paused while she waited for this tantalising piece of information to sink in. Sandy twitched his whiskers, a sure sign of his undivided attention. Jeremy was only partly interested in what Blanche was saying, because he couldn't really concentrate. Now, he had developed pins and needles in the pad of his right front paw and he wanted to shift his position to try and get rid of them.

All he could think about was how he was going to transfer his painful paw from beneath his stomach and keep it concealed from Blanche and Sandy at the same time. Could he shove it under the nearby 'Welcome' doormat without anyone noticing? But as he was trying to work out how to do this, the significance of what Blanche had said hit him. For once, his obsession with hiding his front paws was pushed to the back of his mind. He forgot his pins and needles as the implications of her words sank in and he lifted his head so he could hear her more clearly.

Blanche went on in a conspiratorial voice saying, 'Lucy's parents keep going on about Lucy travelling to a strange place and living there.'

'What do you mean?' Sandy squeaked.

At the sound of Sandy's voice, Jeremy started to giggle. Blanche ignored his tactless tittering and carried on explaining things. She told them that Lucy's mother had become a bit emotional and kept going on about security and suitable accommodation. She also told them that Lucy's mother had started to talk softly to Lucy about keeping safe and eating regular meals. 'Sometimes, she ends up crying,' Blanche confided in a low voice.

Sandy looked thoughtful and then shrilled, 'That reminds me of the time when our boy Robbie went away for a long time.' In an attempt to cover Jeremy's giggling, Sandy started to speak faster, making his voice sound even squeakier. Determined not to be put off by the way his voice was performing, or Jeremy's behaviour, he continued to try and help Blanche out. 'Chris, our other boy, went away too, but that was after Robbie and there wasn't so much fuss that time.'

Blanche felt that she was making progress here and could barely contain her excitement, 'I remember them going, but where did they go?'

'I'm not sure,' Sandy answered, 'but they came home sometimes.'

Blanche looked puzzled and asked Sandy why he or Jeremy had not gone with them. 'I don't know about Jeremy, but I didn't really fancy it,' Sandy answered. 'Anyway,' he continued, 'I was never that close to the boys. I didn't share the same values with either of them.' Then, after a short silence, he added, 'As a matter of fact, I still don't.' It was obvious that there were issues about The Cat Code of Loyalty to People here. Blanche made a mental note to explain the details of the code to Sandy when she had time.

Something else to add to her to-do list.

Blanche sighed. If things had not been so urgent, she would have asked Sandy to explain what he meant by his intriguing comments about values, but she did not want to get side-tracked again. Besides, her relationship with Lucy was different. They had always been much closer than Sandy and Jeremy and their boys. The idea that she and Lucy could be separated because they did not share the same values was unthinkable. If Lucy was going somewhere, then she was going too, there was no question.

The three of them fell silent, then suddenly Jeremy said shyly, 'I know where they went.'

'Who?' piped up Sandy? His thoughts had wandered from

Blanche's problem to his relationship with Robbie and Chris and then on to the reasons why certain dynamics developed between cats and people.

Jeremy gave a superior little smile and said, 'Robbie and Chris of course.'

The effect of this piece of information on Blanche was electrifying. 'Where, where?' she squealed. In her excitement, she suddenly sounded like Sandy. Quickly realising that Sandy might think she was making fun of him, she dropped her voice. It was so easy to destroy a cat's self-confidence. But Sandy pretended not to notice Blanche's slip-up and the moment passed.

In a more measured tone Blanche asked, 'Where do you think they went Jeremy?'

'They went to one of those places where I think Lucy must be going,' he answered smugly.

Blanche frowned; she was not sure how to carry on. Strictly speaking, she should know everything that happened to the cats and people in the Close. But she didn't know anything about where Robbie and Chris had gone and if she admitted it, she might damage her image. On the other hand, she needed to find out as much as she could about her own and Lucy's future. She decided to take a chance and hope that Jeremy and Sandy wouldn't work out that she didn't have a clue what she was talking about.

She coughed politely and pressed Jeremy further. She desperately needed to get him to tell her more. Keeping her voice as calm as she could, she asked, 'What sort of place do you mean?'

Jeremy gave an impatient sigh and said, 'A university of course.'

'Ah yes, I thought so,' Blanche replied. Then, trying to sound as if she already knew the answer, she asked Jeremy what he thought a university was.

Jeremy did not like being put on the spot and he began to look uncomfortable. He bit his lower lip nervously. He wanted to chew the claws on his front paws, but this was out of the question for obvious reasons. He decided that he would tell Blanche what he knew about Robbie and Chris and their time at university as quickly as possible. After that, he would be free to go off to rub his front paws together to stop his pins and needles coming back without anyone watching him.

'I think there are lots of places called universities and some young people are sent there for a long time to be taught things by teachers and be sick,' Jeremy gabbled.

'What are you talking about?' Blanche spluttered. 'Young people go to school to be taught things and what's all this about being sick?'

'I know they go to school,' said Jeremy in a slightly shaky voice. He was becoming more and more worried about being questioned. He gulped and added, 'They go to university when they are older, when they do not go to school any more. They eat and sleep there as well as learning things.' Jeremy then took a deep breath and tried to explain about young people being sick at university. 'When they have finished learning things for the day, they go to special places called pubs and drink special drinks and then they are sick. I think they do it to make themselves feel better. They are just copying us really.'

'Copying us, copying us! What do you mean copying us?' Blanche was convinced that Jeremy's answers about university life could not possibly be true, could they?

Jeremy could see that Blanche suspected that he might be making everything up and he tried not to panic. He took another deep breath and went on quietly. 'They have seen us eating grass to make ourselves sick when we have upset stomachs. They know it helps to make us feel better again so they do it too. I think learning things gives them upset stomachs and I'm fairly sure that's when they drink the special drinks. They make themselves sick, the way cats do and then they hope that they will feel well again.'

Blanche and Sandy were dumbfounded. They stared at Jeremy

goggle-eyed. Jeremy immediately realised that things were not going well, he had gone too far. He had given Blanche and Sandy far too much information, plus, he had made himself sound like a know-it-all. This was a mistake, especially in front of Chaircat Blanche. He hadn't meant to sound like a show-off. After all, he had only repeated what he had heard Robbie and Chris saying. He had assumed that a cat, as intelligent as Blanche, would know a bit about university life. What had he done?

It was time to leave, he definitely did not want to say anything else or answer any more questions. With an exaggerated yawn, he announced that he was feeling a bit sleepy and he fancied going for a little stroll to clear his head.

He began moving from his squatting position so he could stand up. But standing up in company would reveal his front paws so he quickly adopted his special strategy for dealing with this particular problem. He stretched out his back legs and used them to propel the rest of his body around in a circular movement.

Then, with his bottom pointing toward Blanche and Sandy, he carefully unfolded his front paws. This way, he managed to keep them out of sight as he drew himself up to his full height. Keeping his back toward them, he looked over his shoulder and called, 'See you later.' Then he tried to look unconcerned by strolling away and whistling softly. This would have worked if Jeremy had not tried to stroll with a kind of pigeon-toed walk. But he couldn't help it; it was the only walk he could manage and keep his front toes hidden as he went on his way.

With Jeremy's sudden departure, Blanche felt at a loss. She wasn't sure what to do next. Perhaps she should take some time to sort herself out. Too many thoughts were going through her mind and Sandy didn't seem to have anything more to add to what had already been said. She decided she would have a little snack and then doze by the pond in her peaceful, sunny back garden until it was time to eat again. Later on, she would try to make more sense of the unbelievable things she had heard from Jeremy. Blanche got up and gave a farewell nod to Sandy and he nodded in response. She padded back down over the adjoining lawns and jumped back onto her windowsill.

The information from Jeremy had left her feeling very confused. She was so confused that she had to stand on the edge of the windowsill for a moment or two because her mind had gone completely blank. Half-in, half-out, she had to think about where she was going and why she was going there. Suddenly, an unexpected whiff of warm wind tickled her tail and her misty mind cleared. Of course, she was going to get a snack and then make her way to the back garden.

She went to the utility room and chewed the few biscuits which were left in her red and white food bowl but she didn't really taste them. She finished them off anyway and, burping loudly, she shouldered her way through the cat flap in the back door. She walked over the grass and made herself comfortable on a warm bit of paving at the edge of the pond and tried to loosen up. Closing her eyes, she lifted her face to receive the shafts of thermal gold sent by The Great Cat God of Light and Warmth and listened to the fountain gently playing on the surface of the fan-shaped water lily leaves in the water.

CHAPTER 5

Georgio

As Blanche began to unwind and feel more herself again, a blast of music suddenly shattered the peace of the garden. It made her jump and completely spoiled her chances of relaxing. She knew straight away who was responsible and glared in the direction of the greenhouse. The culprits were Georgio and Helena and they were totally unaware of the black looks Blanche was giving them. To be fair, they were so involved with what they were doing in the greenhouse that they hadn't noticed Blanche by the pond at all. Blanche didn't care, she was in a bad mood now and she carried on glaring at them. When they eventually picked up on the glare and realised that Blanche was giving them dirty looks because their loud music had annoyed her, they both shouted, 'Sorry, sorry, sorry!' and Helena quickly turned the music down.

But the more Blanche stared at them, the more she had a problem keeping a straight face. In spite of herself, she began to smile and her mood started to lift. She couldn't help being amused by the picture that Georgio and Helena made because they were such a strange pair. Georgio is a fifty-year-old tortoise and Helena is a slug (nobody knows how old Helena is). Georgio has lived in the garden since Lucy was born and everyone knows that he has been going through a sort of mid-life crisis lately. One grey morning, Blanche had overheard him confiding to Helena that he wanted to change the way he lived his life. He wanted to take chances and he told her that he had decided to break free from his boring routine because it was time he experienced some danger and excitement.

Georgio was brought to the UK from a faraway place so he doesn't speak in exactly the same way that everyone else does. But on that grey morning, he did his best to make Helena really understand how he felt. 'Every days I does the sama thing. I eats the sama food; I walks up and down on the sama grasses and I shelters from the sun and rains under the sama bushees. In the winter I hibernates ina box ina the shed and ina the springs I wakes up and does the sama as things over and over again. It's alla so safa, I have no surprises amigo.'

Helena understood exactly what he was saying to her and she was very sympathetic. She knew all about having ambitions and wanting more from life and now she had found someone else who felt the same way. She wriggled with enthusiasm, 'We can do something together; we can build a different future. I know we can change our lives and I promise that I will find out how we can to do it. I will make it happen.' Filled with enthusiasm, Georgio gazed at her with shinning eyes and they did their best to high-five each other.

But Georgio was not a fool and knew that he didn't have a lot of choices. Deep down, he knew that he was stuck in the garden and would probably spend the rest of his life there. If he was going to do something, it would have to be on his home turf. But knowing this didn't discourage him. It only made him more and more convinced that he had to broaden his horizons, even if it meant that that those horizons were confined to the garden. He was determined to follow his dream and have a go at doing something new and risky before it was too late.

Then, out of the blue, he and Helena came up with a brilliant idea. One beautiful afternoon, Georgio was trying to find something more interesting to do. He was pacing around the garden furniture for the third time on the trot and he was seriously bored. He was really glad that it was sunny, but that didn't stop him feeling dissatisfied with his humdrum existence. He was just thinking about working out his frustration by stamping on a daisy, when Helena slithered up to him. 'Look, look,' she hissed, 'look at what Andrew is doing.'

'Whata deed you say?' Georgio wanted to carry on with his daisy stamping and didn't pay much attention to her.

Beckoning him to follow her, she hissed again, 'Look, look!'

'Hokay, hokay.' Sighing, Georgio decided to leave the daisy alone and do what Helena wanted. After all she was going to help him change his life and it wouldn't be a good idea to ignore or upset her at the moment

Andrew was sitting under a parasol near the pond. Although he was on his own, he was chattering and pointing excitedly at his laptop. He was watching a boy windsurfing across a lake at a tremendous pace. Lurching forward, Georgio glanced at the picture on the screen and what he saw stopped him in his tracks. He could not believe his eyes. The speed at which the boy was travelling was amazing. Georgio felt his heart jump with joy; here was his answer. Normally, speed was not something that tortoises did. Georgio was born knowing that he would never be able to achieve anything faster than a quick march; but in that spectacular split-second everything changed for him.

Almost crying with happiness, he shouted, 'Hah! thees ees eet, I hev founded the way. Hi will be the firstest tortoise ina the world to go fastest, hah!' He had never felt so excited as pictures of himself dashing across water flashed before his eyes. He looked at Helena, she looked at him and they both jiggled from side to side and punched the air.

Since that moment he had become determined to windsurf across the garden pond and he would do whatever it took to make it happen. He was convinced that this was a dream he could make real. He knew it was not going to be easy, but he had told himself that nothing was going to stand in his way. He would begin to prepare now, today. It was essential that he made a start before he had to hibernate for the winter.

He usually hibernated when it started to get colder and the sky got dark in the afternoon. Georgio knew that there wasn't much time left but surely there was enough time for him to find out what sort of training and equipment he needed and where to get it. If he started to prepare and train now he would be ready for his first trial run next spring. He also knew he would need a lot of help, especially from Helena, but that shouldn't be a problem. Hadn't she already promised to do everything she could to support him? Of course, rumours of Georgio and Helena's plans became big news in the garden, causing all sorts of speculation and sensational gossip to spread like wildfire.

Sitting by the pond and thinking about Georgio's plan, Blanche couldn't help thinking how very lucky Georgio had been. If he had not met and made friends with Helena he would never have discovered how he could be the fastest tortoise in the world. Sometimes, it was strange how things worked out. Who would have thought that an exceptional slug like Helena and a daredevil tortoise like Georgio would end up in Wells, let alone in her garden?

CHAPTER 6

The Wise White Cat and the New Slug

Thinking back, Blanche remembered how Georgio and the local cats had been mystified at Helena's appearance in the garden. They had not been sure where she had actually come from or why she had turned up, let alone why she looked the way she did. Hearing reports of a fantastical stranger sitting under a plant near the greenhouse, Blanche went to investigate. What she saw was so incredible that she didn't believe her eyes. She knew that she should call an immediate meeting of the CAALE to discuss what she had seen but she needed to think and talk things through with The Wise White Cat first. Hurrying to find him so she could tell him about the exotic, bizarre, astonishing, peculiar, sluggy thing that had just arrived on her territory, Blanche dashed out into the Close. The Wise White Cat was sitting under the majestic, chestnut tree that grew at the side of Jeremy and Sandy's house. He was very still and looked like he was meditating.

Blanche didn't like to disturb him, so she just gave a polite cough and waited for him to notice her.

Slowly, he turned his head and smiled, 'You wish to speak to me Chaircat Blanche?'

Blanche couldn't wait to give him all the news about the newcomer but she had a problem trying to get The Wise White Cat to follow what she was saying. The foreigner looked like a slug but she couldn't really compare her to the other slugs in the garden because he or she wasn't exactly like them. The thing was, he or she seemed to have arms and hands. As Blanche tried and tried to describe him or her, she ended up talking faster and faster, saying the same things over and over again.

Slowly shaking his head and holding up a paw, The Wise White Cat stopped her. 'Do not race your words against the wind. If you do not communicate clearly, how can others learn from you?'

Slumping down on the grass, Blanche sighed, 'Sorry, 'I know, I know.'

The Wise White Cat put a paw on her shoulder, 'I will now go to your garden alone and talk with this sluggy thing. I will also search for the truth by using my special mystical powers to communicate with The Great Cat Gods and I will tell you of the knowledge they give me.'

Blanche thanked The Wise White Cat and settled down to wait for him to come back. As he walked away, Blanche couldn't help noticing that he hadn't cleaned his bottom properly that morning. There was a small bit of poo poking out of his fur; it was about the size of a baked bean. A little slip of poo protocol here, she thought. For a split second, Blanche wondered if she should tell him, or should she let him walk around like that all day? She decided not to say anything; he was a very proud, dignified cat and she wasn't going to be the one to upset and embarrass him.

As she stared at the bit of poo dangling from his bottom, she tried really hard not to laugh. It was no use, and once she started she couldn't hold back. She laughed and laughed until her sides hurt. Pressing her paws over her mouth, she hoped The Wise White Cat wouldn't hear her. Blanche knew she had to get a grip, but it was no use; every time she tried to pull herself together, a great guffaw would burst out. She ended up completely losing control, hooting and rolling around on the grass. Luckily, nobody saw her making such an exhibition of herself.

By the time The Wise White Cat came back, Blanche had managed to get hold of herself. Little giggles still escaped from her mouth, but she covered them up by pretending she had hiccups. She had to keep looking at his face because if her eyes strayed towards his bottom she knew that she would explode with laughter again.

'I have spoken to the new slug and I have received messages of wisdom from the Great Cat Gods and I have much to tell you.' As he spoke, The Wise White Cat noticed that Blanche was acting a little strangely. Her eyes were wet and her jaws were clamped too tightly together for her to answer him. She just nodded and he could hear little moaning sounds coming from her. What was the matter with everyone this morning? Coming across a few of the other cats earlier, he had noticed that they seemed to be acting strangely too. As he was making his way to the chestnut tree, he even saw one mother quickly clamping a front paw over the mouth of her young son.

Ignoring Blanche's odd behaviour, The Wise White Cat stood as close as he could to her so nobody else could hear what he was saying. Blanche felt a little uncomfortable because she didn't want to be anywhere near that bit of poo hanging from his bottom. Casually, she edged around so that she couldn't see or smell it.

Speaking in a low voice, he told her what he had found out from other residents of the garden and by tapping into his mystical powers. 'The new slug is a female called Helena and what you say is true. She has arms and hands, making her very unusual. She is the only slug in the UK who can trace her family back to a group of slugs known as Sluggitus Armarallius.' He paused and then added, 'These particular slugs started to appear on the earth at the same time as the dinosaurs did.'

'The what?' Blanche was beginning to feel that she was going mad. A slug with little arms and hands that lived at the same time as things called dinosaurs?

Seeing her shock and confusion, The Wise White Cat went on to explain, 'Dinosaurs were enormous reptiles that...'

Before he could finish explaining Blanche completely lost control and grabbed The Wise White Cat by his chest fur. Shaking him, she yelled, 'Reptiles, reptiles! What's "reptiles"?'

Forgetting that he was supposed to teach the other cats about peace and love, The Wise White Cat roughly pushed Blanche away and growled, 'Take your paws off me and behave yourself. You don't really need to know about dinosaurs and reptiles so let's forget about them, shall we?'

Blanche nodded quickly, she couldn't believe what she had just done. 'Sorry, sorry, I'm under a lot of stress at the moment,' she stuttered.

The Wise White Cat bowed his head. 'I accept your apology, now let us forget it and move on. 'According to my information, the people, who have studied these particular slugs, think that they originally came from South America. Of course, the most interesting thing about them is that they have two arms and two hands. This makes them far more skilful than other types of slug.'

Pausing again, he was relieved to see that Blanche had calmed down and seemed to be herself again because he had lots more to tell her. 'They can use their arms and hands in many different ways and for many different purposes. They use them to push themselves forward when they are moving from one place to another. They also use them when they are feeding. They can actually pick leaves off plants and hold them to their mouths as they eat. But most surprising of all is the way they use their arms and hands when they play. They arm-wrestle with each other and some of the stronger slugs can even do proper wrestling. They can also use their arms and hands to throw small pebbles in the air like balls and hit the pebbles with tiny sticks.'

'Are you joking?' Blanche didn't want to offend The Wise White Cat, but surely what she was hearing couldn't possibly be right, could it?

'No, I do not joke Chaircat Blanche and I have not come to the end of the slug knowledge yet.'

'There's more?' Blanche croaked.

The Wise White Cat took a deep breath. 'The people who study slugs think that there aren't many Sluggitus Armarallius left because they spent too much time wrestling and playing with pebbles. They should have hidden themselves from their enemies instead of enjoying games so much. But there are still a few who have survived and they turn up in different places across the world. Now, one of them has arrived in your garden.'

The Wise White Cat tried to look as if he wasn't completely staggered by what he was telling Blanche but the truth was that he was also totally bewildered. He couldn't come to grips with the reality of a slug with arms and hands either. The wisest of cats who had ever lived would never have thought it was possible. The world was a truly mysterious place.

'Well!' Blanche blew out her cheeks and stared at him, she was lost for words. The Wise White Cat could see that she was having a real problem processing the information. She opened her mouth to say something but then closed it again when nothing came out. He sat down to wait until she was ready to speak; he wasn't going to risk rushing her. Apart from anything else, he didn't want to be attacked again. As he sat down, the fur around his bottom felt distinctly squishy. He got up again and turned to check it out. He was horrified to see a bit of squashed poo had been smeared over the top of one of his back legs.

He goggled at the smear, 'What's that?' he said sniffing it. Then, it dawned on him what had happened and he gave a loud groan of despair. Had he really been walking around like that all morning? He had to find somewhere private to clean himself immediately. 'I've got to go!' he gasped and galloped off as fast as he could. Blanche watched as he fled, crashing into some bushes as he scrambled over the garden wall.

Putting a front paw on her chest, Blanche copied the solemn way The Wise White Cat talked and announced to nobody in particular:

'Ah well!
When The Wise White Cat finds poo on his fur,
He doesn't want to cause a stir.'

Chuckling, she wondered how long it would be before he would be able to look her in the eye again.

CHAPTER 7

Helena

Of course, Blanche wasn't the only one who couldn't believe her eyes when she first saw Helena. On the day she showed up, it didn't take long for word to get around. The whole community buzzed with reports of a momentous happening. An astonishing slug with arms and hands was sitting under one of Andrew's hosta plants. Most of the resident slugs said they didn't believe it, but that didn't stop them slinking over to have good look. Although she was nervous, Helena smiled and waved at them. 'Please, please let them like me,' she repeated over and over to herself.

In a panic, the resident slugs drew back together in a huddle and just gawked at her and then at each other. What was this creature? Helena smiled and waved at them again. Then, it dawned on her that perhaps waving at them wasn't a good move. They didn't have arms and hands so they couldn't wave back. Had she offended them when that was the last thing she wanted to do?

Very, very slowly, they edged toward her and looked her up and down, carefully checking her out. Yes, she was one of them, yet she was not the same. Helena waited patiently. She hoped they would accept her because she liked the look of this garden, especially the hostas. In the end, curiosity got the better of the resident slugs and they overcame their apprehension. They introduced themselves and when the introductions had been completed they relaxed and couldn't wait to bombard her with questions.

She answered them with so much charm that they pushed away any remaining fears and prejudices they may have had. Not only that, they agreed to invite her to join them as a member of their garden group without any further cross-examination. Once it got around that the resident slugs had accepted her, everyone else wanted to make the acquaintance of the most extraordinary creature they had ever seen. Even the CAALE decided that she would not have to go through any further form of investigation before she was accepted by them as a member of the garden community.

Helena was relieved and grateful for the generous way she had been made to feel at home. There and then she made up her mind to make a real effort not to act as if she was different. She knew that her arms and hands might make the other slugs uneasy or jealous so she wouldn't make a big thing of them. But she wouldn't try to hide them either because they were great for doing so many different activities such as keeping herself strong and healthy. It occurred to her that here was an ideal opportunity to use them in a way that would benefit others. Perhaps she could help her new friends to be stronger and healthier too. It would be her way of saying thank you to them. Delighted with this idea, Helena made up her mind to act as their fitness instructor, offering to set up keep-fit exercise classes in the greenhouse as soon as possible.

The exercises she would teach could only be for the chest, back and arms; she couldn't include legs because she didn't have any. She made it clear to all the animals and insects in the garden that the classes were not just for slugs, everyone was welcome to come along, even earwigs and worms. She explained that doing a few body movements every day would give them a feeling of well-being and more energy. Sadly, her message didn't get through because nobody turned up for the first two or three sessions and she ended up doing her exercises on her own. Helena was disappointed at the poor turnout, but she did not give up. She was sure that she would think of some way of persuading at least some of the habitants of the garden community that regular exercise was good for them.

Then she had a stroke of luck. Just by chance and for no

particular reason, she asked Georgio about the black, square thing she had noticed under one of the bushes in the garden. He told her it had been there a long time and it played music when you pressed the buttons. Georgio had a very good memory and he remembered Lucy calling it an MP3 player. Georgio also remembered that he had stopped his stroll around the garden one afternoon to watch Lucy press the buttons to make it work.

Helena held up one her hands and gave him a confused smile, 'But Georgio, my friend, the square thing does not have any buttons.'

'Ah amigo! That isa becausa eet ees ina a leetle case and hyou take eet outa the case and pressa the buttons to play eet.'

He said that he didn't think anyone had opened the case for many, many days because Ellie, Clare and Andrew's little niece, had said it was old and thrown it into a bush and everyone forgot about it. Georgio sighed and rubbed his head as he told Helena how amazed he was as he watched Lucy pressing the buttons on the player to make music come out.

Helena went very quiet as she listened to what Georgio had to say. Then, to his complete surprise, she gave a long thoughtful whistle and began tapping one of his front legs with her right hand. He didn't know what he was supposed to do so he just tapped his other leg on the ground in time with her taps. But it soon became clear that Helena wasn't paying any attention to him or their tapping. Helena was obviously deep in thought about something else and wasn't aware of what she was doing. Suddenly, she gave a little jolt, stopped her tapping and burst out, 'I am onto something big my friend.'

She waggled her fingers at Georgio and told him that she could press buttons and if she managed to get hold of the MP3 player and open the case she would be able to use it in her sessions. Music would make all the difference in the world. But her high spirits didn't last long because Georgio asked her how was she going to get it to the greenhouse? Helena hung her head and shrugged. He was right she couldn't drag the MP3 player all the way to the greenhouse; she just wasn't strong enough.

But one night not long after she had told Georgio about her brainwave, she had another inspired idea. One of Ellie's small roller-skates was lying near a sun lounger; she had probably forgotten to take it home. Helena waited until the people in the house had all gone to bed, then she used her strong, little arms and hands to pull the MP3 out of the bush. She flexed her arm muscles and dragged it over to the skate and using all her strength, levered it onto the skate and slowly, she started to push it across to the greenhouse. It took ages and it was nearly morning by the time she finally rolled it through the door and onto the concrete pathway that ran between the wooden shelving on either side. After tugging and gripping the case, she managed to prise it open and, with a little grunt of satisfaction, she flopped down on the cool strip of concrete, panting. She was worn out, but she was a very, very happy slug. Now, she was in business and grinning broadly, she patted the MP3 player's buttons over and over again.

Once she had worked out which buttons to press on the MP3 player, she started to choose the best music for each of her exercises. She was sure that her selection would make everyone want to join in. However, there was one problem she hadn't thought about. Although working-out to music would be a great new experience for her, she had forgotten that the sound of music would not be a new experience for her new friends. They were used to hearing it blaring out, especially in the summer. Clare, Lucy and Andrew played music all the time when they were sunbathing, having a barbeque or just hanging out in the garden. She could only hope that the music she played would turn out to be popular and get everyone in the mood for exercising.

As it turned out, Helena was right to be worried and her worst fears came true when she turned on the MP3 player for her first musical workout. The songs she chose to play didn't get the kind of reaction she had hoped for. No queues formed at the greenhouse door, nobody even made an inquiry. On the whole, everyone was polite enough, except for one or two of the snails who made a few whispered, niggling remarks about the tracks that she had chosen. Luckily, Helena didn't hear them, she was too upset to pay attention to what they, or anyone else said. But the thing that hurt her most was the fact that Georgio hadn't shown up.

She couldn't even cheer up when she had seen some of the animals do a few dance steps in time with the music as they passed by. Others even sang along to some of the songs, but they did not actually come inside the greenhouse to take part in her class. Finally, Helena had to admit that using the MP3 player was not going to be enough to get them through the door. She almost felt like giving up and, dropping her head in her hands, she had a little cry. But Sluggitus Armarallius are not quitters. With a determined twist of her head, she pulled herself together and made up her mind to try harder, but how?

Blanche had been around at the time and she had seen how depressed Helena had been over the musical setback and she felt really sorry for her. It wasn't difficult to see how much Helena wanted her sessions to be a success; her heart was obviously set on it. Seeing her slumped against a plant pot trying to work out what to do, Blanche had decided to help out. She joined her in the greenhouse and cleared her throat to get her attention. Then, crouching beside her she had asked kindly, 'Do you mind if I make a suggestion?'

'No, not at all, I need all the help I can get,' Helena gulped.

'Well, have you thought about the way you look? I know that there are special clothes for fitness instructors. Perhaps you would be more successful if you wore the right outfits, things like sports vests and crop tops with matching head and wristbands.'

Helena didn't answer for a long time. She had been told that Blanche was a clever cat, but what she was saying sounded silly. How could she get hold of an outfit small enough to fit her? 'Um, thanks, but I don't think I'll be able to find anything in my size.'

Blanche had a twinkle in her eye, 'You leave that with me.

Which colours do you like best?'

Helena gave Blanche a shy smile. 'I know that soft violet and pale blue suit me.' Blanche winked at her, 'I think I will have a nice surprise for you in a couple of days.' 'What? How?' Helena wasn't sure that Blanche was serious.

Blanche tapped one of her front paws against her nose and leaned forward. I'll just say, 'IPAD, ONLINE and Andrew's CREDIT CARD.' Helena didn't have a clue what Blanche was talking about. But, before she could ask her to explain, Blanche had left. Helena just caught sight of her as she trotted across the garden and disappeared through the cat flap into the house.

Blanche kept her word and, two days later, she turned up in the greenhouse carrying a tiny parcel in her mouth. Dropping the parcel in front of Helena she pointed a paw and said, 'This is for you.'

Helena clapped her hands together. 'For me?' Blanche nodded. Helena tore the parcel open and gasped. She couldn't believe it, Sports vests, crop tops, headbands and wristbands, all in her favourite colours and, more importantly, in her size.

'Wow! Thanks so much!' She couldn't wait to try on her new outfits and when she did, she felt as if all her dreams had come true. Her reflection in the panes of glass in the greenhouse showed a truly sporty slug. Surely, now her classes would be a smash hit with somebody; but deep down she hoped that Georgio would be the first to join up.

To be fair, Georgio had been amazed when he saw Helena using the MP3 player. He couldn't work out how she had managed to get it to the greenhouse all on her own; nevertheless, he was full of admiration for her strength and determination. As he watched her pressing the buttons, he wasn't quite sure what she was doing. He thought she might be busy getting used to working the player so he decided not to disturb her; he would tell her how impressed he was another time.

But when Blanche told him how upset Helena had been when nothing happened at her first musical exercise class, Georgio felt awful. He did a quick march to the greenhouse straight away. He reached the open door but was stopped in his tracks when he saw her warming up in one of her new outfits. She looked stunning standing on a tall plant pot that had been turned upside down; moving in time to the music, she was every inch the professional. It was easy to see that she knew what she was doing. As he watched Helena, it occurred to Georgio that if he was going to be a successful windsurfer he would need to get in shape himself and he would have to start doing some serious workouts. Helena's keep-fit class seemed to be the perfect answer.

When she saw Georgio staring at her, Helena smiled and waved, 'Come in, come in,' she was a breathless so this seemed a good time to take a break. She turned the music down and sang out, 'Hello Georgio, would you like to join in?' She didn't want to sound too pushy in case she frightened him off. 'I think you will enjoy it and you will feel much healthier after you have done a few sessions. Who knows, a bit of training might help you to be a better windsurfer?' Why, oh why hadn't she thought of this before? She held her breath as she waited for him to answer.

'Allo Helena, I theenk I want, yes, but I theenk I want to ask manya questions pleese. Is okey?'

'Of course, ask as many questions as you like.' Helena wasn't sure, but sometimes, she thought he sounded like some of the older members of her family. How strange. Perhaps he came from the same faraway place as they did; it was a small world.

Firstly, Georgio reminded her of her promise to help him with his surfing ambition. Secondly, he asked her if she could show him how to build up his strength. He also asked her how she had got her outfits and did she think it was possible a get a wetsuit like the one the boy was wearing on TV in his size. Georgio paused and then asked if she could also give him some advice about getting a small surfboard as well. Helena couldn't get her words out fast enough, 'Yes, yes, I can show you what to do and I know a cat who will help us to get you what you need to wear and a surfboard.'

'Thees is good, Georgio's eyes shone with excitement. 'Who

ees thees cat and can thees cat helpa me find a leetle surfboard?'

'Yes, yes, you know her, it is Chaircat Blanche and she seems to know all about getting anything you want from somewhere called ONLINE.'

'Hah! Thees is very, very good,' Georgio wagged a front leg at Helena. 'Okey, lets us goa now, show me howa to be healthy tortoise.' Helena was ecstatic and she turned up the music as she began to put him through his very first workout session.

The next time she saw Blanche, Helena explained what they were trying to do and asked her if she would be able to help Georgio get hold of a wet suit and a small surfboard. Blanche was impressed with their energy and ambition and it was good to see Helena looking as if she had all her old spirit back. She told them that she would be glad to get hold of the things that he needed. It took a bit longer to sort out Georgio's gear, but it arrived at last and she delivered it to him in the greenhouse.

When Georgio saw it, he thumped his legs on the ground and yodelled loudly. With Helen and Blanche helping him, he tried on the wet suit and was thrilled that it was a perfect fit over his shell. Then, he scrabbled onto his surfboard and he pretended to surf. Laughing and cheering, Helena helped him to stay steady. When he began to get a bit too ambitious and started to slip off they decided it was time to stop. Together, they hid his new things underneath a roll of old hosepipe until he was fit enough to practice using them properly.

Once he had started the sessions, Georgio had to learn how to pace himself. Helena had to slow him down because she didn't want him to damage any of his muscles. Then he found that some of the movements were difficult because he needed to make his legs stronger and his shell made it hard for him to do full leg movements. Helena tried to show him how to work his legs but, not having legs herself, she had to use her arms to do it. He was disappointed that he couldn't move his front legs as quickly as Helena moved her arms, plus he couldn't even move them in the same way as she did.

Chapter 7 – Helena

'Oh noa! I can't do eet, I can't do eet,' he wailed and looked as if he was going to give up.

'Yes, you can,' Helena shouted, 'we will just do it a different way.'

This meant that Helena had to design a special leg exercise programme for Georgio. She slowed her arm movements right down and concentrated on working Georgio's front legs up in the air and lowering them again. She also had to think of a way he could practise some back-leg exercises. She couldn't do them herself, so she just had to call out what he had to do. She persuaded him to thrust his back legs in the air as he was lying upside down on his shell. Of course, this was a very scary thing for him to do because he didn't feel safe when he was upside down. Anything could happen and he wouldn't be able to get back on his feet on his own.

At first, he would complain, 'I don like thees, I don theenk it ees a good idea.'

Helena smiled patiently and gently talked him through it. 'Trust me, you will be fine. Just work those legs, work those legs.' Then, after he finished, she always helped him to get back the right way up. She would push her strong, little arms under his shell and help him to get back on his feet. After a while, Georgio started to get used to his special exercise programme and his legs began to show some defined muscle tone. He was so pleased with everything that Helena was doing for him that he started telling everyone how amazing she was. Eventually, everyone in the garden had to admit that Helena's tortoise workout programme was showing some real results.

With a start, Blanche realised that she had been lying in the same position for far too long. She stretched and shifted as she continued to watch Helena and Georgio. They were thrusting their arms and legs backwards and forwards and sideways in time with the music. As usual, Helena was positioned on top of her tall plant pot, demonstrating the moves and shouting out instructions.

'Front arms and legs up, up, up, up, higher now. Let's thrust these arms and front legs up higher. Up to the sky, Georgio, up to the sky.'

Georgio was following every instruction brilliantly. Now he was standing upright, on his back legs, working his arms and then his neck and head. He was moving well to each beat of every song and Blanche was pleased that things seemed to be turning out so well for them. Remembering how she had helped to make it all possible, she gave herself a little, mental hug. Sitting by the pond waiting for the session to finish, she wondered if they might be able to help her in return. Maybe, and it was a big maybe, there was a slim chance that they could shed some more light on the Lucy/university mystery?

CHAPTER 8

Possibilities

As she waited, Blanche, spotted Back Shed again; he hadn't gone home after all. He was dozing, sprawled out on her flat garage roof. He was not a pretty sight with his head flopping to one side and his tongue hanging out of his mouth. She stared at him as, sloppily sucking his tongue back in his mouth, he stretched and looked at her with a mischievous glint in his sleepy eyes. She knew that he knew that she wasn't happy about him hanging around her house and garden. She knew that he knew that he shouldn't be anywhere near the Close and he definitely knew that he shouldn't be on her garage roof.

She hoped that The Great God of Light and Warmth would make the garage roof too hot for him and he would burn his bum and leave, but it didn't happen, he didn't move. He just tapped his paws in time with the music coming from the greenhouse until he nodded off again. Just when was he going to get the message and realise that he wasn't welcome by any of the adult cats in her area?

As he continued snoozing on the garage roof, Back Shed started to dribble and snore and Blanche couldn't bear to look at him any longer. Turning way, she yawned and thought that perhaps she should have a little catnap herself while she waited? She wasn't sure how long she slept, but when the music stopped, she woke up and opened her eyes. Helena was packing up her things, chatting and joking with Georgio. It was obvious that he was worn out but he was laughing happily. Blanche stood up and arched her back. She gave herself a little shake and approached the pair. When they saw her coming over, they started to make their way out of the greenhouse to meet her.

'Have you had a good session?' Blanche called out to them.

'Yes, theenk you,' answered Georgio happily. He took a sip

from the saucer of water that Helena held out to him and wiped his forehead with the small, brown hand towel. It had been a free gift that had arrived with his wet suit.

'Georgio really tried his best today,' Helena enthused. Although she sounded a bit breathless, it was obvious that she couldn't wait to tell Blanche how hard Georgio had worked. 'I think he is amazing and he is making excellent progress,' she added.

Georgio laughed modestly, 'I jest wanta to do my best, I wanta to be ready for my beeg challenge.' Chuckling, he glanced at Helena and playfully nudged her right shoulder.

Chuckling with him, Helena nudged Georgio back, 'Oh you will be, my friend, you will be. But none of this would have been possible without Chaircat Blanche. We would not have got this far without her help support, would we?'

'Ah Chaircet Blanche, how can whee ever theenk you?' Georgio's small, bright, brown eyes twinkled as he lowered his head and bowed to her.

Blanche smiled at them graciously, 'Good, good, glad to have helped.' She was pleased that things seemed to going so well for them but thoughts of Lucy, university and moving away were still uppermost in her mind. Surely this was the perfect opportunity to find out if Helena and Georgio had heard anything on the garden grapevine. It was a long shot because they were not particularly interested in garden gossip. Of course, that meant that it was unlikely that they had much to tell her. Without expecting to learn anything new, she decided quiz them anyway. That was when she noticed that Back Shed had lifted his head. Suddenly, he was wide awake and was watching what was going on. When he realised that he had been spotted he waved a podgy paw and clambered down from the garage roof to join them.

Blanche sighed, this was the last thing she needed. She wanted to keep her problem low-key but Back Shed just couldn't keep his mouth shut. Although he had been rejected by CAALE, he tried to worm himself in by getting involved in everyone's business whenever he could. He repeated all kinds of gossip to the CAALE members who would listen. There had been numerous times when he had caused terrible problems with his wild scandalmongering. It's true that some of what he said often had a grain of truth but he would add his own sensationalist titbits just to make himself the centre of attention.

Helena and Georgio were looking at Blanche, waiting for her to speak. It was clear that she was about to say something important but what was it? Blanche hesitated, on the one hand she thought she should forget the whole thing but on the other hand she just couldn't let it go. Taking a deep breath, she made up her mind to go for it. For better or for worse she decided to talk to them, even if it was in front of Back Shed.

As he reached them, Back Shed sensed that something big was in the air and he could not hide his excitement. His whiskers, ears and tail all twitched at the same time and he couldn't stand still. This was not a good sign and Blanche knew she was probably going to regret talking in front him. But, she couldn't put it off any longer; it was now or never.

Quietly and quickly, she gave Helena and Georgio all the information she had about the Lucy situation. She explained how serious it was and how she needed to find out more. She also told them what Jeremy had told her about universities. After she finished nobody said anything. Then, Back Shed rubbed his chin and muttered softly, 'He's right you know.'

'Who is?' Helena asked.

'Jeremy,' replied Back Shed. 'Some young people do go to places called universities to learn more things. But I think that only young people with a pen and a duffel coat are allowed in. An old sailor friend told me about the pen and duffel coat rules a long time ago. When he was young, he lived with some people who sent their children away to a university. I think people call it 'uni' these days. Of course, the rules might have changed,' he added.

Usually, Blanche didn't believe a word that Back Shed said, but this time he did seem to know what he was talking about.

It seemed to make some sort of sense. Besides, Lucy had loads of pens and coats. She probably had a duffel coat somewhere so getting into this university would not be a problem for her. But Blanche wasn't sure that she would get in. She was pretty sure she could lay her paws on a pen but could she get hold of a duffel coat. What was a duffel coat anyway and what did one look like? If she didn't know, she couldn't even order one online

Then, to her relief, Back Shed explained. 'Some of the people I sailed with used to wear duffel coats.' They are warm coats, with a hood and little wooden pegs, called toggles. The toggles hold the coat together at the front.'

'Hwhy do theeya needa them?' asked Georgio.

'I am not absolutely certain,' said Back Shed unexpectedly. It wasn't like him to admit that he wasn't absolutely, a hundred percent sure about everything. 'Perhaps it's to stop people catching fleas from each other. Maybe human fleas can't get through the thick material. I expect that's why duffel coats have hoods, he went on.

Blanche's shoulders slumped. Just where am I going to get a duffel coat?' she mumbled to herself. Getting her own pen was easy enough; there were pens in every room in the house. But a duffel coat for heaven's sake! Now that she knew it was a thick coat with a hood, perhaps she could order one online after all. But what if it didn't fit properly? She didn't know how to send things back to exchange them. That particular problem had not occurred to her when she ordered Helena's and Georgio's outfits. Luckily, they had been perfect fits so it hadn't become an issue.

As if reading her mind, Back Shed tweaked her right ear. 'Don't worry lovey,' he said soothingly. 'I know where we can get you a duffel coat. Oh yes! But it will take some planning though,' he informed her in a low, dramatic voice.

Helena and Georgio were clearly dying to know what was going to happen, but they had to go and do their winding-down exercises after their session. Seeing that Georgio was reluctant to leave Helena took charge and insisted. 'We have to do them my friend if we don't our muscles will hurt and won't work properly tomorrow.'

'I know amigo, but do we haff to go back to thee greenhouse now?'

'Yes, I'm afraid so, come on.' As they went, they kept looking over their shoulders, hoping to catch a few more words of Back Shed's plan.

Blanche and Back Shed watched them go. Blanche looked confused and unhappy but Back Shed had a knowing, shifty air about him. He knew he would have to try really hard to convince Blanche that his duffel coat plan would work. Of course, he already had his own reasons for helping Blanche. If Blanche left with Lucy, then her position as Chaircat of the CAALE would be vacant and there would be big changes. Who knows, perhaps even an outsider like him might stand a chance of being voted in as a member of the association.

'Look,' he said, trying to sound as if he really cared about Blanche's problem, 'I think we should have another meeting with Jeremy and Sandy. They know a bit about young people going away and Jeremy even knows a bit about universities.'

Blanche had to agree that it did seem a good idea but she had to think it through. She asked Back Shed to wait while she went for a quick drink. She squeezed through the cat flap in the back door and stood over her silver water bowl in the utility room. As she took a sip of water she caught sight of her reflection. 'What am I doing?' she muttered to herself. 'What on earth am I doing? I must be losing my mind even thinking of listening to Back Shed.' Then she shook her head and squared her shoulders. What choice did she have? Deciding that she really had no choice, she gave the cat flap a violent punch before striding out into the garden to rejoin him.

'When do you think we should have this meeting?' she asked him.

'How about now,' he replied. 'No time like the present. I know it's nearly lunch time, but let's go and see if Jeremy and Sandy are free, shall we?'

CHAPTER 9

Preparing for Action

Jumping over the garden wall, they made their way over to Jeremy and Sandy's house. For reasons known only to himself, Back Shed started mincing alongside Blanche and chortling, 'Don't you think their green and orange window blinds are a complete nightmare?'

Blanche looked daggers at him; did he really think she was going to be drawn into a stupid conversation about the colour of window blinds today? Besides, Jeremy and Sandy had just come into her line of vision and she didn't want them hearing Back Shed's waspish remarks about their soft furnishings. It would only cause offence and make things awkward. But they didn't appear to have heard anything and were still sitting in their usual position, on either side of their front door. They looked at each other in dismay as they watched Back Shed coming toward them with Blanche following behind. Surely they were not together. Usually, Blanche avoided Back Shed like the plague.

'Hi sweeties,' Back Shed called as he saw Jeremy and Sandy glaring at him. They knew that he only called them sweeties to wind them up. He loved annoying them if Blanche was around. He thought it was hilarious because they really couldn't say anything in front of her in case she marked them down as over-sensitive trouble-makers.

'What does he want?' Blanche heard Jeremy hiss to Sandy between clenched teeth. 'Who knows?' Sandy squeaked softly. 'Perhaps he will go away if we pretend we haven't seen him,' he added.

But when it became clear that Blanche was actually with him, they immediately became alert. Sandy stretched up to a sitting position but Jeremy remained lying down. He definitely had to keep his front paws hidden from view. If Back Shed noticed them he would only begin teasing him the way he always did and start singing that song 'I Am What I Am'; he really knew how to press Jeremy's buttons.

'Look,' Blanche glowered at Back Shed as she waved a friendly paw at Jeremy and Sandy. 'Don't start anything with Jeremy today. Don't mess him about with any of your usual shenanigans, okay?'

'I don't know what you mean, lovey.' Back Shed giggled, 'I'm always on my best behaviour when I'm with you.'

'You had better be,' muttered Blanche threateningly.

When they reached Jeremy and Sandy, Blanche explained that she just needed a bit more information about universities if possible. Jeremy and Sandy looked blank. All they could do was apologise and explain that they had told her everything they remembered, they just couldn't tell her anything else.

'Okay, okay,' Back Shed took over. 'We will just have to work with what we have got. It will all be fine,' he added. 'First things first, let's focus on getting the things our Blanchey Baby needs to get into a university.'

'Don't call me Blanchey Baby,' Blanche spat at him. 'I am the Chaircat of the CAALE and I deserve some respect.'

'Whoops! Sorry your majesty,' Back Shed pretended to be scared and he gave her a trembling bow. Unfortunately, he accidentally bumped his head on one of the heavy, ornamental plant pots by the front door.

Blanche, Sandy and Jeremy all burst laughing. Blanche gave a great guffaw and Jeremy laughed so much that tears ran down his cheeks. He nearly uncovered one of his front paws to wipe his eyes, stopping himself just in time. Although Sandy thought it was hilarious, he could only manage a piercing trilling sound.

Back Shed did not know where to put himself. He tried to cover up his pain and embarrassment by tossing his head back and running his right, front claws through the thick fur around his neck. But he didn't fool anyone because they had all heard him whispering, 'Ouch!' under his breath. Then he became annoyed because they wouldn't stop jeering at him and shouted, 'It's not that funny, let's move on!'

Still weak with laughter, Blanche, Jeremy and Sandy made an effort to do as he asked. But then Jeremy gasped, 'That's what you get for calling us sweeties,' and that started them off again.

Back Shed couldn't take any more and exploded. 'Enough!' he yelled. He hated making a fool of himself; it wasn't good for his image. His tail started thrashing the ground, as he became more and more hot and bothered. Realising that things were getting out of hand, the others pulled themselves together with difficulty. They tried not to look at each other; after all, this was supposed to be a serious conversation and a lot depended on it.

'Right,' Back Shed said, pulling himself together and taking charge again, 'let's address the duffel coat problem first. We have got to get hold of one that will fit Blanche. We can't have her turning up at this university looking like a she's wearing someone else's clothes, can we? Now,' he added without waiting for an answer, 'I know Blanche won't mind me saying this, but she is not one of the slimmest cats in the Close.'

But Blanche did mind and she gave Back Shed a filthy look. 'Are you saying I'm fat?' she spluttered. 'Talk about the pot calling the kettle black.'

'No, no,' Back Shed replied hurriedly. 'Not at all. You have a good body shape for your age.'

In a huff, Blanche repeated after him in a thunderous voice. 'For my age!'

Sandy couldn't believe his ears. Back Shed was beyond belief. Trying to show Back Shed he should stop making insensitive, personal remarks about Blanche's weight and age, Sandy quickly made a cutting gesture as he drew one of his front paws across his own throat. This was completely lost on Back Shed and it looked like he was going to carry on digging himself into a hole. Jeremy and Sandy groaned, although Sandy's groan sounded more like a light hum. Back Shed had done it this time. Didn't he realise that Blanche would have him for this? Aware that the situation had to be salvaged, yet again, Jeremy took his courage in both hidden paws and intervened.

'We all know that Blanche is in the peak of condition, but that doesn't solve the problem, does it? Duffel coats are made for people not cats. At least I've never seen a cat wearing one, have you?' he asked the others.

Forgetting her huff for a minute, Blanche shook her head sadly. 'No I haven't, this whole situation is all too much, it's impossible,' she faltered.

'It's not!' Back Shed crowed. 'That's what I was trying to tell you earlier. I know where we can get one to fit you, just listen. I often go for a stroll in Wells High Street and I know the shops pretty well. One of the shops sells toys and they put some of the toys in their shop windows.

This was fascinating stuff. None of the cats from the Close had ever been as far as Wells High Street and they had never seen any of the shops. They knew what shops were because they had seen them on television, but actually coming into contact with real shops was almost beyond their imagination. They were stunned into a rapt silence.

At last, Back Shed had his audience in the palm of his paw. He was the centre of attention and he was going to make the most of it. 'Guess what is standing in the middle of one of the toyshop windows?' he asked playfully.

The others just shook their heads. 'A bear,' he sang out triumphantly. 'A bear,' he repeated, 'a lovely, little, furry bear.'

Clearing his throat, Jeremy tried to make sense of this piece of surreal information. 'I don't see…' he began. But Back Shed cut him off before he could finish.

'Guess what the lovely, little, furry bear is wearing?' he asked. Not waiting for an answer, he delivered his bombshell. 'The lovely, little, furry bear is wearing a blue duffel coat, I think he's supposed to be famous or something. Anyway, his blue duffel coat will be perfect for Blanche, right size, a hood, everything.'

With a self-satisfied smirk he added, 'All we have to do is go and get it.'

Blanche, Sandy and Jeremy could not have been more dumbfounded if he had told them that there was a live pigeon, doing back flips, in the toyshop window.

Back Shed was so pleased with himself that he couldn't resist getting up on his two hind legs and dancing round and round in a circle. 'The bear is wearing a big, floppy hat and wellington boots as well,' he sang out as he danced. 'But we don't need those, do we?' he gasped breathlessly. The dancing was beginning to wear him out and turn into a stagger. He decided to drop down on all four paws before he fell over and made a fool of himself again. But, he wasn't completely out of breath because he asked smugly, 'Am I a genius or what?'

While all this was going on, Little Treasure had appeared on the front path of her house. She was watching Back Shed and grumbling to herself. 'What did that nincompoop think he was doing? Dancing about like a great clown. He hasn't got a clue about paw work or timing. Everyone knows that I'm the one and only dancing cat worth watching around here, not that heavy-pawed lout.'

His attempt to dance really touched a nerve. The very idea that someone like Back Shed should even try to encroach on her position as the dancing diva of the Close was completely out of the question. She made up her mind that she would go and put him in his place. As she walked purposefully over to the others, she was aware that everyone had turned to stare at her. Of course they had, she was beautiful.

But as Little Treasure reached the group, she realised that they were indeed staring at her, but not in admiration. Something else was in the air. 'What's going on?' she demanded.

The others just looked back at her.

'Well, what's going on?' she repeated peevishly.

In the end, Back Shed couldn't resist the opportunity to show off and he outlined his master plan. Little Treasure started sniggering at the preposterous suggestion of her mother wearing a coat. The sniggering became hysterical howling as a picture of Blanche, showing off a coat on a catwalk, lodged itself in her mind. Tears streamed from her eyes and the hair mascara in her right eyebrow began to smear as she wiped the tears away. Then, it was Back Shed's turn to giggle as he pointed to her smeary face and told her that she looked like a panda. Little Treasure's hysteria quickly turned into violent anger and she picked up a twig and rushed at him shrieking, 'Don't you laugh at me, you, you big plodder.' Alarmed, Sandy backed away from the skirmish and looked as if he was going to leave. Not for the first time that day, things were spinning out of control.

Suddenly Blanche's voice cut through the air like a knife. 'Pack it in at once,' she commanded in her most authoritative, Chaircat manner. Back Shed and Little Treasure stopped glaring at each other and Little Treasure hurriedly dropped her twig. 'That's better,' said Blanche. 'You know how I hate physical violence.' And with that, she promptly cuffed Little Treasure around the ear. 'Now, are we going to put this plan into action or not? Plus,' Blanche went on, 'are we going to let Little Treasure be part of it if she wants to be?'

'Why don't we ask her,' suggested Jeremy timidly.

'Good idea,' Blanche replied and she gave Little Treasure her full attention. 'Now, do you want to be involved or not?' she asked. Little Treasure looked a bit baffled but she nodded even though she didn't have the remotest idea what they were talking about. 'Right then,' Blanche continued, 'that's settled but you have to understand that you can't drop out if you get bored and you can't confuse things with any of your silly ideas. Is that clear?' Little Treasure again nodded her lovely head in agreement.

'Can I say something?' Sandy shot Back Shed an enquiring look. 'Just how are we going to get hold of this duffel coat?'

'Piece of cake,' Back Shed responded confidently. 'We all go down to the toy shop late at night. We climb in through the open toilet window at the back of the shop while one of us keeps watch. Then, we grab the coat from the bear and come back here.'

'But how do we know the toilet window will be open?' Sandy persisted.

'It's always open,' Back Shed answered. 'I know because I have jumped through it loads of times.'

'That's all very well, but how do we know that the toilet door will be open so we can get into the rest of the shop?' Blanche asked.

'Good point, good point,' said Back Shed expansively. 'But don't you worry, my captain. The catch on the toilet door doesn't work properly. All the door needs is a bit of a push and "Hey Presto!"'

Everyone looked at each other. To be fair, Back Shed seemed to have thought of everything, except one teensy-weensy little thing. He hadn't taken on board the fact that none of them had ever been to the High Street, let alone seen the outside or inside of a shop for real. Silence descended, as each cat tried to work out how they felt about this enormous challenge. Yes, they were scared. Yes, they were not even sure if it was all going to work. They could even be about to risk their lives if the worst happened and they were run over by a careless motorist. Were they absolutely sure that they were ready to take such a risk?

Except for Blanche, none of the cats were particularly brave. Yet, yet along with the fear they felt, they also experienced an unexpected thrill of excitement. Could they really carry out such a courageous operation to help their respected and beloved leader?

After a long silence, Jeremy suggested that they take a vote, the cats all nodded in agreement. 'All against; raise your right, front paw,' he whispered in a nervous voice. With a sinking feeling in his stomach, he immediately realised what he had done. To vote, he would have to expose a disfigured paw. He could have cried at his own stupidity. 'Hang on a minute,' he whimpered, 'I'm not sure about using paws to vote. What about just saying yes or no?'

Blanche wasn't having any of this, she had quickly worked out what was going on and decided that the time had come for Jeremy to confront his paw inhibitions once and for all. She turned to him and gently asked, 'Do you want to be included in all this?' Jeremy nodded. 'Then,' Blanche continued, 'you know that you will have use both of your front paws sensibly when we go to the toy shop, don't you?' Jeremy nodded again. 'Well,' Blanche went on, 'don't you think that this may be an opportunity for you to try and face up to your fears and try to get over them?' Almost sobbing, Jeremy nodded for the third time. 'Right then, call for the votes again.'

Jeremy felt as if he was going to be sick but he took a deep breath and repeated, in a shaky voice, 'All against; raise your right front paw.' Little Treasure quickly raised her right front paw but then, just as quickly, lowered it when she realised that she was the only one with a paw in the air. The others frowned at her. It came as no surprise to them that she didn't really understand the voting system.

'All for?' Jeremy asked in a hoarse voice. The tension was palpable. This time, all five front paws were raised including Jeremy's, and a yes vote was accepted and passed. Jeremy could hardly believe what he had just done. He looked shell-shocked as he lowered his paw and cleared his throat. In a shaky voice, he announced that they would carry out Back Shed's plan and finalise the details as soon as possible. The other cats gave Jeremy a loud cheer and Blanche clapped him on the shoulder. Back Shed unsuccessfully tried to hug him and Little Treasure actually managed to give him a kiss on both cheeks. Sandy simply grinned from ear to ear. Acknowledging the cheers from his friends, Jeremy gave his most bashful smile and proudly waved his right paw in the air once more. Another cheer went up, even louder than the first.

After taking part in such an important decision, plus witnessing Jeremy's emotional breakthrough, they all felt drained. Blanche said that it would be a good idea to suspend things until after

lunch and meet up again later that afternoon. They would all feel refreshed and be ready to brainstorm ideas. Everyone agreed and she declared the meeting closed. As Blanche and Little Treasure made their way back to their house. Back Shed followed them. 'Um, would it be possible to share your lunch?' he asked with one of

his smarmy smiles. Blanche gave him a long, knowing look. He was such a user, but to be fair, he did come up with the only plan that had a chance of helping her out.

'Oh all right,' she agreed, 'but don't scoff it all.' Back Shed gave a snort of pleasure and the three of them crowded around the food bowls in the utility room to eat lunch. Both Blanche and Back Shed ended up with bits of food all over their whiskers because it was difficult to share Blanche's bowl without getting messy. The fact that they kept jostling each other out of the way so they could get to the tastiest bits of food first didn't help. In the end, they both looked as if they had been using cat food and biscuits as some sort of facial scrub. Back Shed had even managed to get some in his left ear.

Little Treasure was disgusted at the state they were in. She gave a disdainful sniff as she daintily ate her own lunch from her own bowl. She was about to eat her last biscuit when Back Shed belched and she caught a whiff of his smelly breath. Crying, 'Ugh!' she jumped as far away from him as she could and, covering her face, she suggested that they should all go off separately and have a rest.

Catching a bit of the whiff herself, Blanche agreed and made her way upstairs and settled down on Lucy's crumpled duvet. Bits of cat biscuit and cat meat dropped from her whiskers onto the duvet cover. Thoughtfully, she licked the cover clean, then tucked her head between her front paws and tried to put all her troubles to the back of her mind.

Still belching, Back Shed thrust his way out through the cat flap and curled up on a sun lounger in the back garden. Little Treasure had intended to go through the cat flap into the garden to reach her favourite spot, just inside the open patio doors. But she didn't want to follow him outside in case he made any more smells. Instead, she decided to take the route from the utility room into the kitchen so she could reach the dining area and the patio doors that way. She was tired so she was glad that nobody was around to waylay her; she had the place to herself. Reaching her usual sunny, patch of carpet, she gave a lazy yawn and, with one flowing movement, gracefully arranged herself in the most fetching position for a beauty sleep.

CHAPTER 10
The Plan

Back Shed was the first to wake up when Lucy came banging in through the back gate a couple of hours later. He opened one eye and watched as she went into the house. It looked as if she had been swimming because her hair was wet and she was carrying her sports bag. She was in a hurry and didn't notice Back Shed on the sun lounger.

Surprisingly, she didn't notice Georgio either, puffing away as he slowly shoved a folded garden chair across the lawn.

After Lucy had disappeared inside, Back Shed shook himself fully awake and stared at Georgio. Back Shed wasn't easily impressed, but he had to admit that pushing garden chairs across grass must be very tiring work for a small tortoise. He was even more impressed when Georgio gave him a cheery wave.

'Thees eesa good fora my training,' he panted.

Back Shed had to hand it to him, Georgio's positive attitude and his commitment to his training programme was impressive; even inspiring. Not to him, of course, nothing would ever inspire him to do anything that involved strenuous exercise. He was a traveller and a philosopher, not an athlete. Suddenly, and for no apparent reason, he rolled off the sun lounger, stood up on his back legs, threw out his front paws and tilting his head at the sky, proclaimed, 'I'm the one and only true cat philosopher in the whole of Wells.' Pausing, he added, 'and everywhere.'

After leaving Lucy in her bedroom texting one of her friends, Blanche was emerging out of the cat flap when she heard Back Shed's proclamation. She gave a loud snort and burst out, 'In your dreams.' Back Shed couldn't think of a quick response so he just sniffed, pursed his lips and turned his attention back to Georgio.

'Where's Helena, why isn't she training as well?' he shouted to him.

'Ah, my amigo, Helena, she no training with me now, she lika to taka siesta under lavender bush thisa tima day.' Just as Back Shed was going to say something about Helena dodging out of afternoon training and taking advantage of Georgio's gullible nature, he changed his mind. Best not to wind Georgio up in front of Blanche at the moment. She wouldn't think it was funny and she might see it as an opportunity to have another go at him for stirring up trouble.

But Blanche had lost interest in Back Shed's philosophical pretentions and anything else he might have to say. She was more concerned with getting everyone together and working out a viable plan and simply asked him, 'Where's Little Treasure?'

'She's still fast asleep inside, she hasn't moved from the carpet in the dining area.'

Blanche pushed past his sun lounger and stuck her head inside the open patio door. Seeing that Little Treasure was in a deep sleep, she reached in and shook her until she started to stir.

'What's up, what's up?' Little Treasure whimpered through half-closed eyelids.

'For heaven's sake get a grip,' Blanche growled back. 'We are supposed to be meeting up with Jeremy and Sandy to have a brain-storming session and work out a plan,'

'What now, this minute?' Little Treasure complained.

'Yes, now!' Blanche bawled impatiently. 'Come on!'

Reluctantly, Little Treasure got up, stretched and sleepily followed Back Shed and her mother to Jeremy and Sandy's house. She was feeling grumpy because she didn't like being hauled out of the house before she had time to check how she looked in the bathroom mirror. Hurriedly, she smoothed the fur on her head and face as best she could before anyone else had the chance to see her looking rumpled.

Jeremy and Sandy were already waiting for them. But, before they got down to business, Sandy suggested that they needed somewhere more private for such an important meeting. Outside his and Jeremy's front door was a bit public and Blanche's garage door was shut. So they all agreed to move into the little wooden summerhouse at the bottom of Jeremy and Sandy's back garden.

Luckily, the door was not closed properly and Sandy kicked it open with one of his sturdy back paws. They went inside and made themselves as comfortable as possible on the slightly musty chairs and cushions. Hesitating outside, Little Treasure refused to enter the summerhouse. 'I'm not going in there,' she complained, 'it's too smelly.' Jeremy and Sandy tried not to look offended and Blanche was mortified. Casting her eyes downwards, she apologised to them for her daughter's bad manners.

Rousing herself, she muttered, 'Give me strength,' as she manhandled her inside and sat her down on an old, tartan travel rug in the corner.

'Ow! No need to push me so hard,' Little Treasure whined, 'that really, really hurt.'

'No it didn't,' Blanche answered through clenched teeth.

'Yes it did and you have ruined my face fur.' Little Treasure began to cry and edge towards the door. 'I want my little piece of blue velvet,' she sobbed. 'I want it, I want it.'

'That's enough!' Blanche warned. 'You will sit where I put you and be quiet. You will forget about your face fur, your piece of blue velvet and stop crying. If you don't, you know what will happen.' Then, she whispered the magic words in Little Treasure's ear, 'Home Perm!' Miraculously, the crying stopped and, with a theatrical, shuddering sigh, Little Treasure settled down on the travel rug.

After witnessing such an embarrassing scene between mother and daughter, nobody knew what to say. Taking advantage of the awkward silence, Back Shed took the opportunity to speak first.

'I'm not trying to take over,' he said unconvincingly, 'but I think it might be a good idea if I run the meeting because I am the only one who knows the way to the toy shop in the High

Street.' Blanche wasn't sure about this. After all, she was the Chaircat of the CAALE. On the other hand, he did have a point. Blanche thought about it for a few seconds and then reluctantly decided it was probably for the best.

'Right!' she said, 'that's okay with me. How does everyone else feel about it?' There were slow nods of agreement all round and Little Treasure sneered slyly to herself. For once, her bossy mother would not be in control of everyone and everything.

'Now, I declare this meeting open,' announced Back Shed, banging his paw on the wooden floor. Unfortunately, he banged it a bit too hard and he had to suck his paw knuckles to relieve the pain.

'Typical, good start,' Blanche blew out her cheeks in exasperation and slowly head-butted one of the doorposts.

But Back Shed wasn't going to be put off by a piddly bit of sarcasm and he carried on regardless. 'I have given this plan a lot of thought over the past couple of hours and I propose we do it in stages. Stage one is as follows: the first thing you all need to know is how to get to the High Street, so you will need directions. Once we are in the High Street it's easy to find the toy shop because all we have to do is keep going in a fairly straight line.'

'Do you think you should draw us a map?' Sandy suggested.

'Yes, yes, good idea,' Back Shed agreed and with that he went outside and came back with a thin stick. 'We are here,' he said as he drew an X on the dusty floor. Concentrating as hard as he could, he drew a line from the X to show the way out of the Close into The Avenue.

'I know that way,' Little Treasure shouted triumphantly.

'Yes, but we need to know where to go after The Avenue, don't we?' Blanche pointed out. 'None of us has ever been further than The Avenue, have we?' she looked at Little Treasure accusingly. 'At least, we shouldn't have, especially you. Have you been further?' she pressed.

'No, no,' Little Treasure answered hurriedly, 'no mum, I

haven't, honestly, I haven't. Um!' Blanche looked sceptical.

'Now,' Back Shed went on, 'listen carefully. When we get out of The Avenue, we turn right and walk down to Wells Cathedral. We know what it looks like because we can see it from Blanche's back garden. 'You have to admit, it's gorgeous, isn't it? Lovely statues and towers and things. Plus, it's very big, so we can't miss it. Anyway, it's here,' and he marked another cross on the map. 'Then, we go across the Cathedral Green and take a few steps under a kind of old, stone porch into the Market Square, and then we cross the Market Square and we are in the High Street.' He placed a further cross to show where the old, stone porch was. Satisfied, he gave a huge grin and began to draw the final line from the top of the High Street to the toy shop.

He was obviously getting carried away and pressed on his stick with too much force. With a snap, it suddenly broke in two and Back Shed was left holding a mangled, twiggy stump in his paw. 'Its fine, it's fine,' he reassured everyone, 'the last bit of the map is just another straight line and I can draw that with the bit of stick that's left, see?' With a flourish he completed the map and bowed to his audience. 'Don't forget,' he added, almost hugging himself with self-importance, 'I will be leading you all the way.'

'Ur, shouldn't there be another cross to show where the toy shop is?' Jeremy asked with a worried frown, 'and what happens when we get there?'

There were mumbles of agreement.

'I haven't finished yet,' Back Shed lied petulantly and he rapidly marked the map with another cross. Preparing himself to outline stage two of the operation, he stood erect. Taking a deep breath, he adopted a serious expression. 'Everyone focus,' he began and he looked at Little Treasure to check that she was still paying attention. It didn't look like it because she was smiling and patting a dandelion head on the floor. 'Treasure, lovey,' he cooed with exaggerated patience, 'this is very important. Do you think you could try to stay with us?'

Little Treasure quickly shot a guilty glance at her mother and Blanche gave her a warning glare, 'I am listening, honestly I am,' she simpered.

'Well make sure you are,' everyone chorused.

'Let's move on, let's move on,' Sandy chirped. He was getting a bit fed up with all the distractions and he wanted to hear the rest of the plan.

'The toy shop is here,' Back Shed pointed to the last cross on the map. 'When we get to the shop, I will guide you from the High Street down a narrow passage, at the side of the shop, to the open toilet window at the back. One of us should stay outside to keep watch. The rest of us will jump through that window and make our way through the shop to the windows at the front. The bear with the duffel coat is in the middle of the window closest to the passage. We will wrestle the coat off him and Blanche will try it on for size.'

'Do you think the bear will put up much of a fight?' asked Little Treasure nervously.

'No, no. It's not real bear, it's just a toy,' laughed Back Shed. Privately, he hoped he was right. He tried not to think about the possibility of wrestling with a live bear in the middle of a toy shop window, in the middle of Wells High Street. He quickly brought the subject back to Blanche. He hoped this would stop anyone else pressing him further about live bears and fighting.

'Blanche should keep the coat on until we get back to the Close. It is the only way we can get it here in a fit state. If we try to drag it, it will get dirty and the people at the university might not let Blanche in with a dirty coat.' Back Shed's plan did seem well thought out, but there was a problem that bothered Jeremy.

'What about those toggle things that fasten the coat?' asked Jeremy. 'How will we get the coat off the bear if we can't unfasten it?' It was a good question, opening fastenings on clothes was not something that cats ever had to do.

'I can do that,' cried Little Treasure, 'I can do that, I have had quite a lot of experience of chewing things off bedspreads, I can easily chew a toggle off a duffel coat.' While it was true that she did have experience of chewing things off bedspreads, it did not necessarily mean she could work out how to chew off a toggle. Noticing that the others didn't look convinced, Little Treasure drew back her shoulders. She was not going to be discouraged from her one chance to prove herself. 'I can do it and I will,' she said solemnly.

Blanche's mouth fell open in dismay. Was this her empty-headed daughter talking? Did Little Treasure just come up with the possible solution to a tricky problem and was she really going to try and solve it all on her own? Blanche had to admit that the answer was yes and, for the first time in her life, her chest swelled with parental pride. She wasn't used to this kind of feeling rushing through her heart and tears came to her eyes. Hiding this display of emotion from the others, she pretended to cough. She cleared her throat and decided that this was probably a good idea to bring things to a close. 'On that note, I think we can congratulate ourselves on a very productive meeting,' she announced with obvious satisfaction. 'We have covered everything we can for now.'

However, Back Shed was a bit put out by the way Blanche had suddenly taken over. He had run the meeting and he should be the one to close it. He wasn't prepared to let her have the last word, even if she was the Chaircat of the CAALE. 'Um, one more thing,' he gabbled, 'just when are we going to put this plan into action?' There was a stunned silence as the others tried to come to grips with the answer to this weighty question.

Now he had everyone's attention again, he went on in a more measured tone, 'I am aware that Blanche does not know when she and Lucy are actually going away to university so, I propose that we carry out the plan as soon as possible. Blanche should be prepared for the move in plenty of time. What he said made sense, but the question, of when they were going to carry out the plan, remained. He coughed and continued, 'I suggest that we do it tonight. After all, I'm already here in the Close and the information will still be fresh in our minds,' Back Shed added smoothly.

'Another thing we should remember is that, if we leave it for too long, the toy shop might sell the bear or move it from the window and put it somewhere else. We might not be able to find it and then what would we do?' He was sure that all his impressive logic made sense to everyone else so, he proposed another vote. 'All against going tonight, raise your right front paw,' he boomed out in his best ceremonial voice. Not a paw was raised, not even Little Treasure's. 'All in favour of going tonight?' Back Shed boomed again. But only four front paws went up this time.

Jeremy's paw had started to go up, and then it was slowly lowered again. It wasn't because he had slipped back into feeling sensitive about his front paws; he was just feeling a bit unsure about how quickly things were moving. He found himself blurting out, 'Don't you think we should take a little more time over this? It's alright for you,' and he pointed at Back Shed accusingly. Now Jeremy had actually overcome his font paw inhibitions it seemed as if there was no stopping him using them at every opportunity. It seemed as if he was even prepared to use them to make forceful gestures to express himself. 'You know the High Street. The rest of us have no idea what it's like down there. You are fully aware that it will the first time we have ever been further than The Avenue?' He stopped and looked thoughtful. 'Before we go perhaps we should have some sort of training day?' he suggested hopefully. They all groaned loudly, even Little Treasure knew that training days were a complete waste of time.

'Don't be ridiculous!' Back Shed snapped. 'I've told you I will lead the way and I've drawn a map. What more do you think we will learn from a training day?' he demanded. Without waiting for an answer he went on, 'Training days are stupid, you have to tell the group of cats why you are there. Then, you have to do those ice-breaker things and fall backwards hoping that cat will stop you falling on the floor. It's supposed to teach you about understanding and trust. What's the point?' he asked becoming more and more heated. 'We understand why we are here and we trust each other, don't we?' He put his front paws on his hips, tossed his head back and glared at Jeremy. Imagining he looked intimidating, he only managed to look a bit puffed up. He really couldn't do intimidating.

'Well, I just think that we need more time, we don't want it all to end in disaster, do we?' Jeremy snapped back.

Blanche decided that she had better step in. 'I think it will be fine,' she soothed Jeremy. 'I agree that it's always worrying when we cats have to negotiate new territory, but we do have a map and it shows us where the toy shop and the High Street are. A training day will just take up too much time and we do have to get a move on.'

'Oh Okay, okay,' Jeremy reluctantly agreed.

'Let's take the vote again then, shall we?' Blanche asked. She was pleased to see that the vote was unanimous this time and she gave Jeremy a grateful nod of the head. 'Right then, let's meet here when our people have gone to bed and are sound asleep. Be sure to check on that last point,' she ordered. 'One more thing,' Blanche added, 'do not tell any of the other cats in the Close about what's going on; they might want to come with us and that would only cause all sorts of complications. Not only that, I think we should keep the news about my leaving the Close confidential until I have more of an idea about when I am going.' Although, Jeremy and Sandy enthusiastically agreed that they shouldn't tell any of the other cats, privately they were not sure about complete confidentiality. Would Back Shed and Little Treasure really be able to keep such a juicy piece of news a secret?

The meeting then broke up leaving Back Shed annoyed because Blanche had managed to have the last word after all. But he calmed down when he worked out that he could turn this to his advantage. The afternoon was coming to a close and he was getting hungry. The very least Blanche could do was to share her evening meal with him. True, she had shared her lunch but he had worked out a great plan and he had run most of the meeting; she owed him big time.

'Any chance of a spot of dinner?' asked Back Shed casually. 'I could get some food elsewhere but I would have to leave the Close and then come all the way back again.'

'I expect so,' replied Blanche absently. 'Eat as much as you like. I'm not very hungry anyway.' In fact, her stomach was churning with nerves, but she couldn't tell him that.

'You can have some of my food as well,' Little Treasure offered. She was on a roll with her mother and she wanted to keep in her good books. Smiling, Blanche threw her a look of approval. Turning her head away, Little Treasure smirked to herself. She was definitely learning how to stay in in her mother's good books.

'See you later,' the five cats called out confidently to each other as they left the summerhouse. But they were not all feeling confident. Blanche was not the only one with a churning stomach. Jeremy and Sandy were also feeling uneasy. They agreed that they were excited and curious but they also confessed to each other that the whole plan was frightening. Just what were they getting into? Of course, there was no answer to that particular question. That particular question would only be answered after they had taken the plunge and embarked the most daring adventure of their lives.

CHAPTER 11

The Daring Adventure

It was impossible for Blanche to relax as she waited for the adventure to begin. She couldn't make a move until everyone had gone to bed and fallen asleep. Only then could she leave. She always slept in Lucy's bed, but Lucy had taken ages to drop off and she had begun to think that she would never get away. At long last, Lucy started to snore gently and Blanche decided to try and make her escape. But, before she went downstairs, she checked that Clare and Andrew were also sound asleep.

When she went to wake Little Treasure, she was surprised to find her ready for action. Her head was sticking out over the edge of her basket and she whispered, 'Where have you been, I've been ready for ages.'

'It's easier for to you to leave the house without anyone knowing because you sleep downstairs on your own,' Blanche answered. This was true; Little Treasure's sleeping quarters were tucked away on a surface over the central heating boiler in the utility room. Her basket was placed well away from any draughts so it was a warm and cosy snuggery. Her basket was also warm and cosy because it was fitted out with a duvet inside a soft, silky princess cover. 'Look', Blanche sighed, 'I had to hang on until the coast was clear but I'm here now, so let's get going.'

But as Blanche was about to lead the way through the cat flap, she noticed what Little Treasure was holding. It made her stop in her tracks and have second thoughts about taking her along. As Little Treasure had started to climb out of her basket, Blanche looked back and saw that she was clutching her piece of blue velvet tightly to her chest. 'You can't take that,' Blanche hissed as she jumped up onto the surface and tried to wrench it away from her.

Little Treasure tightened her grip and wouldn't let it go, 'I can take it and you can't stop me.'

'Yes, I can, give it to me.' Blanche grabbed the piece of blue velvet and held it in the air.

As Little Treasure lunged to get it she banged her head on the corner of the boiler. 'Look what you've made me do,' she moaned as she sat down on the surface and rubbed her head. I might get a bump now and it's all your fault.'

Quickly hiding the blue velvet at the back of the boiler pipe, Blanche hauled Little Treasure down from the surface. Then she dragged her, snivelling and kicking, to the back door. But as she tried to force her through the cat flap, Little Treasure spread her front paws out over the sides of the cat flap so Blanche couldn't move her. Refusing to be beaten, Blanche flexed her muscles and, with all her strength, grasped her around the middle hurling them both at the cat flap. As they hit it, it broke and bits of plastic and metal fell on the floor with a plinking, clinking sound. Blanche and Little Treasure stared at each other, surely the noise had woken everyone up. They didn't wait to find out. Without another word, Blanche flung Little Treasure and herself through the broken cat flap into garden. So much for making a quiet getaway.

This was not a good start. As she and Little Treasure landed outside the back door, Blanche got the sinking feeling that there was probably going to be a lot more trouble ahead. But then she perked up as she sniffed the air; it was fresh and cool and there was a gentle breeze. In spite of her doubts she decided that this was a positive sign.

Back Shed was waiting for them. He hadn't heard the cat flap noise because he had been hanging around by the greenhouse. He had wanted to pass the time by having a chat with Georgio or Helena. However, Georgio had gone to sleep hours ago and although Helena was wide awake, she didn't seem to be very keen on chatting. When she had woken up after her nap under the lavender bush she was starving hungry so she had gone in search for something to eat. Now, she was greedily tucking into a succulent hosta leaf for all she was worth. She knew she had to be quick because one of the other slugs had told her that Andrew was always threatening that he would do unspeakable things to any slug or snail he caught eating his prized hostas.

Sometimes he even did a night patrol, with a torch. This made hosta leaf meals a risky business. Ignoring Back Shed, Helena stuffed the last bit of a particularly delicious leaf into her mouth. She didn't have the time to talk to him now and she didn't want to anyway. He was such a busy, busy blooming body. She was relieved when saw him walking over toward Blanche and Little Treasure standing outside the back door. Although she was pressed for time, she did briefly wonder what the three cats were doing, together, in the garden at that hour, but she couldn't risk stopping to ask them. She was far too busy choosing the next leaf to eat as quickly as she could.

'Catch you later,' Back Shed called softly to her as he joined Blanche and Little Treasure. For a moment, nobody said a word. Time seemed to stand still as they prepared to go over the wall into uncharted territory. This was it, one last look at the garden before they made their journey into the unknown. Of course, it wasn't exactly unknown to Back Shed, but he still felt the hand of destiny resting on his shoulder. With another last, lingering look at Helena, enjoying her midnight feast, they waved and then jumped up onto the garden wall. Helena's mouth was too full to speak, so she just nodded her head and waved back as they disappeared over the other side and vanished from view.

Jeremy and Sandy were sitting on their front path and they got up when they saw the others emerging out of the darkness. 'Are we ready?' Blanche whispered.

'I think so,' Jeremy answered.

'What do you mean, you think so?' Back Shed burst out, covering Jeremy's face with fine spray of his spittle.

'Shh, shh, be quiet,' Blanche commanded as she flapped a paw at him.

'Sorry, sorry,' Back Shed spluttered as he wiped his mouth. 'Let's go, let's go shall we?'

Without a sound, they padded between the six houses in the Close and turned left into The Avenue. After the short walk down The Avenue, they turned right into Saint Thomas Street. Although Saint Thomas Street was narrow, crammed with old terraced cottages and houses on both sides, it was busy with cars, buses and pedestrians during the day. But now, the street was hushed. Apart from a few leaves rustling as they moved in the gentle breeze, nothing else stirred. This really was untrodden territory to the cats from the Close and they came to a halt as they gazed from the top of the street downward to the way ahead.

'Come on,' Back Shed urged them on, 'there's nothing to worry about as long as you stay on the pavement and keep close to the houses.' He paused and added, 'Under no circumstances go near the road.' Staring at each cat in turn, he demanded, 'Has everyone got that?' They all nodded and waited for him to make a move and lead them forward. In contrast to his usual swaying walk, he adopted a determined, almost military step. He marched forward beckoning them on. 'Let's go guys.'

'Shall we keep close to the cottages as well the houses?' Little Treasure looked around expecting approval for drawing attention to this detail. The other cats pretended they hadn't heard her. Sometimes, it was easier that way, especially tonight, when they had more far important things on their minds. Little Treasure didn't take the hint and pressed on with another ill-timed question. 'Back Shed called us "guys", but I'm not a guy, am I Mum? I'm a pretty girl, aren't I?' She looked at her mother, hoping that she would put Back Shed straight on this point. After all, she had been proud of her when she had solved the toggle problem earlier. Surely she would proud of her for picking up on his obvious mistakes.

'You don't have to be a girl to be pretty,' Back Shed retorted. 'I know some boy cats who are quite pretty.'

'No you don't, you're just saying that. Anyway, you're not

pretty, especially when you're asleep. You look horrible then, just like this.' Little Treasure opened her mouth, dribbled and let her tongue hang out sideways.

Back Shed was outraged, but before he had a chance to say anything, Blanche intervened. 'Can you two stop with all this girl-boy nonsense, we'll talk about it later. Anyway, that is not a good look for a beauty icon, is it?' Little Treasure quickly sucked her tongue in and patted her mouth back into shape. Blanche sighed, all this new mother-daughter interaction was wearing a bit thin. 'Now, no more wasting time, what we have to do is to follow Back Shed. 'Pointing at Little Treasure she fixed her with a hard stare, 'You need to keep close to me and stay in front where I can see you.'

The cats began to move down the street cautiously and they looked around at the unfamiliar landscape without speaking. But as they became used to the street, they started to nod confidently at each other and move more quickly. They were almost at the bottom of the street when Little Treasure gave a piercing scream. Terrified, Blanche, Jeremy and Sandy bumped into each other as they stumbled to a stop.

Little Treasure was pointing a trembling paw at the grinning face of a life-sized soldier dressed in a tall, black hat, red jacket and black trousers. It was standing behind the low, stone wall of one of the cottage gardens. 'Who are you, what do you want?' she burbled at him as she got ready to run away.

Back Shed let out a loud guffaw; he couldn't speak for laughing. He laughed until his sides hurt. Little Treasure stared at him suspiciously. 'It can't hurt you, it's made of wood. Can't you see, it's a wooden soldier?' he gasped.

Embarrassed and very angry, Little Treasure leapt at Back Shed and slapped him on the nose yelling, 'Don't you make fun of me, and what's it doing there anyway?'

Back Shed still couldn't stop laughing even as he rubbed his nose and checked to see if it was bleeding. 'It's only a model. It's just there to make the garden more interesting.'

Relieved to hear that the soldier was harmless, Blanche pulled Little Treasure away from Back Shed. She was feeling a bit shaky herself, 'Shh, keep your voices down. I know you have had a big, big fright,' she said soothingly, 'but we have to carry on now, okay?' Even though she still felt scared, Little Treasure gave her mother a wobbly smile. She hung back as she watched the others hurriedly filing past the soldier without looking at him. But when it was her turn to follow, she kept her eyes fixed on his face as she tiptoed her way forward. She wasn't going to take any chances; she was on red alert. If she saw him make even the slightest twitch she would scream and scream and scream. But the soldier didn't move a muscle. He just stood to attention, silently watching, as Back Shed led his band of cats on its way.

Coming to the end of Saint Thomas Street, Back Shed told them to stop. They had reached the point where Saint Thomas Street either turned and curved up towards the Bristol Hill or went right on to the cathedral. Traffic lights had been erected here because it could be dangerous for pedestrians. If they were on the wrong side to get to the cathedral, they couldn't see the cars coming down from the Bristol Hill road as they crossed over. He said they were on the wrong side and had to cross over at the traffic lights to reach the Cathedral Green. Blanche, Jeremy, Sandy and Little Treasure had never seen traffic lights and Back Shed had not put them on the map. Seeing how bewildered they were, Back Shed felt a bit guilty. He patiently explained what they did and told them they could just ignore them at this time of night. As they straggled over the six broad stripes painted on the small crossing, Sandy noticed that Little Treasure wasn't following them.

Fascinated, she had stopped in the middle of the road, and was watching the lights change. Sandy tried to nudge her along, but she seemed rooted to the spot. He called Blanche's name and pointed to her daughter. 'I think we have another situation here.'

'Give me strength,' Blanche muttered as she flopped down on her haunches and sank her head between her front paws.

'A deep breath, Blanchey Baby,' Back Shed was obviously trying his best to show her that he had an empathetic side to his leadership qualities.

'I've told you not to call me that,' Blanche groaned. Then, without another word, she got up, grabbed Little Treasure and brusquely dragged her to the other side of the road and away from the lights.

'Did you see them, did you see them?' Little Treasure babbled excitedly. She had completely forgotten the wooden soldier incident. 'Those lights are lovely colours and they keep changing on their own all the time; it's like magic!'

'Yes, yes, we can all see them, but we can't waste time watching them all night, can we?' Blanche was clearly doing her best to fight the urge to strangle Little Treasure on the spot. She summoned the others to come closer. 'I think we all know that we have a little problem,' she said nodding her head in Little Treasure's direction. 'Any ideas?'

'A little problem, a little problem indeed, are you serious?' For the first time in his life, Jeremy confronted Blanche. 'I don't want to sound unreasonable, but we all know the truth. Little Treasure is a big pain in the bottom and she is slowing us down, Can't we just leave her here and pick her up on the way back?'

Little Treasure started to blink as Jeremy's idea sank in. Would they really leave her here, on her own? Of course, if they did leave her here, it would mean that she could carry on watching the traffic lights.

'No!' Blanche, Back Shed and Sandy burst out together. 'Why not?' Jeremy retorted. Rubbing his chin, Sandy looked thoughtful. 'It wouldn't work. Anyway, chances are she probably wouldn't be here when we got back, then what? Maybe we should take it in turns to watch her for the rest of way, just to make sure she doesn't get scared, distracted or wander off?'

'We don't need this,' Jeremy could feel himself becoming more and more wound up.

'Have you got a better idea?' Sandy demanded shrilly and

when Jeremy frowned and didn't answer, he sniffed and snapped, 'Thought so.' He then waved a dismissive paw in Jeremy's direction, nodded at Blanche and offered to do the first Little Treasure watch. 'She can stay next to me and I'll keep my tail curled around her back so she can't go walkabout.'

Checking to see if everyone agreed Sandy prodded Little Treasure into position. Back Shed returned to his place as leader and the group tramped onward onto the dark and deserted Cathedral Green.

The magnificent cathedral looked foreboding, the figures of saints and bishops, covering the West Front, towered over them. This was no place to dawdle so it didn't take long for them to make their way over the Cathedral Green and pass through the old stone porch into the small, Market Square. The light from four or five Victorian-style lampposts glowed on the cobbles and illuminated the Town Hall and the few shops surrounding the square.

From the Market Square, the cats could see more shops in the High Street which sloped down before them. They looked around in amazement; it was so, so awesome, if only they had more time to explore. Suddenly, their excitement faded away as they all caught sight of it at the exact same moment. It was a shop window full of sparkling rings, bracelets and necklaces. They were instantly aware of the sort of effect this sight would have on Little Treasure and a loud despairing wail of, 'Oh no!' echoed around the Square.

Their worst fears were realised when, before Sandy could stop her, Little Treasure escaped from him and ran up to the shop window. Gazing at the glittering display; her mouth watered with longing. She pointed at a ring, then a necklace, then a bracelet. Finally, she just kept pointing at everything she could see. Breathlessly, she kept repeating, 'Pretty, pretty, pretty,' over and over.

Sandy immediately recognised that this development was serious and should be handled with firmness, care and sensitivity.

If not, it could put the whole operation at risk. However, Back Shed had had enough of Little Treasure's antics. To Sandy's horror, he seized her by the scruff of the neck and pulled her away from the shop window.

'Come on troops, I'll take over,' he commanded. Bending down, he said something in her ear. It wasn't possible to make out what it was, but it must have got through to her because Little Treasure's mouth turned down at the corners and she avoided looking at the others as she nodded her head obediently. What's more, she stayed close to him as they left the Market Square and walked on down into the High Street. To be honest, it was very difficult for the others not to react like Little Treasure and be side-tracked by all the amazing things in the shop windows. But as The Wise White Cat would say, 'When there is a job to be done, nothing should stop the job being done.'

Putting their best paws forward, it only took them a short while to reach the toy shop at the end of the High Street. It was quite a large shop with a window each side of the door. The windows were jam-packed with toys and games. Back Shed steered his band of followers to the first window. Flinging his paw at it he whooped, 'Can you see him, can you see him?' Indeed they could, for there he was, wearing a blue duffel coat with a floppy black hat and red wellington boots. 'He looks very smart, doesn't he?' They nodded gravely as they studied the furry figure standing on the top step of a slide in the middle of the window.

He had a serious, almost disapproving expression on his face. It was easy to imagine that he already knew what they had come for because he seemed to be clutching his coat as close to his body as he could. Little Treasure started blinking again. She was still a bit worried that he might become violent when they tried to steal his coat, but she thought that she had better not risk saying anything else at the moment.

'How do we get to the back of the shop?' Blanche asked.

'We go through that narrow passage between this shop and the one next door. The toilet is at the back and the open window is in the toilet wall.' Back Shed then pointed to a tall, black and gold litter bin on the pavement. 'We can leave the lookout sitting on top of this bin while we are inside. The big question is, who is going to be the lookout? We already know that it can't be Blanche because she has to try the coat on for size. Little Treasure might have to chew off a toggle or two and I think Jeremy will just become too anxious and self-destruct if we leave him to do it. So,' he paused, 'that leaves Sandy.' All eyes turned to Sandy.

'That's me for the lookout then.' He puffed out his chest and smiled reassuringly. He felt good about himself for being so grounded and sensible. How impressed The Wise White Cat would be if he had been there to witness such sound behaviour in such a tense situation.

Now that the lookout question had been settled so easily, Back Shed was ready to take the next step in the operation. 'Shall we make a start?' He moved along the passage. The others followed him as he jumped up over the gate which guarded the back of the premises and landed on the other side.

Standing alone on the pavement, Sandy took stock of the litter bin. The top was slightly domed but it would still be comfortable enough to sit on. He leapt up and positioned himself so he could see the front windows and door of the shop while observing the passage and the High Street at the same time.

'Good luck,' he called softly, as he watched them disappear over the gate. Although he was still feeling proud of himself for being so reasonable, he couldn't help feeling a bit envious. After all, he would miss all the action. But his envy only lasted a few seconds. It turned to relief when he heard Little Treasure complaining loudly that Jeremy had landed on her tail and Jeremy denying it just as loudly. He congratulated himself with a high-pitched chuckle and muttered. 'I think I'm well out of it.'

CHAPTER 12

Inside the Toy Shop

The inside of the shop was like another world, a magical world. Dimly lit by the street lights filtering through the windows, they saw soft toys everywhere, puppets hanging from the ceiling, blown up balloons floating from the handlebars of small bikes, computer games, board games, books, jigsaws, paints, pencils, model kits, dolls and so much more. Giddy with delight, Little Treasure nearly fainted and had to sit down on a plastic toadstool. But Blanche pulled her to her feet; this wasn't the time to be sitting about. With all the setbacks, it had taken longer than she thought to get to the toy shop and if they didn't get a move on, their people would wake up before they got back to the Close.

Back Shed indicated that they should form a line and creep through the shop and up to the front window. He then pointed to the bear, balancing on the top step of the slide. He was staring out at the High Street so he had his back to them. Back Shed made paw movements showing that he wanted them to approach the bear from the rear.

Abruptly, Blanche broke the silence, 'There's no need for us to be quiet or sneak up behind him; he's not real, he can't hear us.' With that, she broke ranks and started to rush up the steps of the slide. Startled into action, Back Shed also launched himself at the steps and tried to push past her. He wasn't going to let her steal a march on him; he was going to make sure that would be the first to get to that duffel coat.

Unfortunately, there wasn't enough room for him to pass her and they both got jammed between the slide handrails. As they yelled at each other and battled to get free, Back Shed accidentally punched the bear with an upward jab. Dislodged from his position, the bear fell forwards and hurtled down the slide.

Still determined to beat Blanche, Back Shed shoved her away from him and tried to follow the bear. Not to be outdone, Blanche grabbed Back Shed's back paw. But Back Shed was not going to be stopped and tugging Blanche behind him, he tried to break away. Almost snarling at each other, they ended up locked in a furious scrum on the top step. Puffing and panting, they both lost their footing and tumbled down the slide, landing in a heap at the bottom, squashing the bear.

The sight of two adult cats behaving like hoodlums shocked Jeremy and Little Treasure. They had never seen any of their relatives or friends behave like this and they didn't know how to react. To make matters worse, Blanche and Back Shed seemed to be having trouble untangling themselves. They were twisting and turning as they rolled around on top of the bear. Jeremy and Little Treasure wanted to help but they were not sure how to separate them. They tried to pull them apart but Blanche gasped, 'Stop!' She was snatching at Back Shed's tail. In the scuffle, it had wrapped itself around her eyes. She pulled it away and bawled, 'Just check to see if the coat has been ripped.'

'Right, right,' Jeremy and Little Treasure turned their attention to the bear and started pulling him away from under them. As they dragged him, facedown along the shop floor, they heard a series of clicking sounds. Without any warning, the bear began to move its head and legs. 'Agh, Agh!' Little Treasure screamed as she turned and ran away. Seeing a doll's pram nearby, she jumped inside to hide. Trembling, she wriggled under a flowery pillow, it didn't really cover all of her but she didn't care. Jeremy couldn't move at all. He just stood there, frantically pointing at the bear and trying to speak. The words refused to come but he continued to open and close his mouth.

Finally managing to break apart, Blanche and Back Shed nervously staggered to where the bear was lying. They couldn't believe what they saw. From the back, he looked as if it was he was attempting to stand up. His head was swinging from side to side and his legs were jerking back and forth. Finding his voice,

TRUCK
MONOPOLY
BLOCKS
TOY CARS

Jeremy managed to gulp, 'Are you okay, we didn't mean to hurt you?' There was no reply. Jeremy was about to try again, when Back Shed suddenly clapped his front paws together.

'Hold on, my band of brave followers, I've seen one of these before. It can't talk and it's not moving on its own. It's a mechanical toy.'

'It's a what?' Blanche snorted.

Back Shed explained that the bear could only move if you pressed a button. With that, he bent down and lifted the back of the duffel coat up as far as he could. He found a small button in the bear's back and with a grunt of satisfaction turned him off.

Completely forgetting about her scuffle with Back Shed, relief flooded through Blanche. 'Good grief, that was a bit of a turn-up. Good job you knew what to do,' she quivered. 'Give me a minute, I need to catch my breath,'

'Let's all take a breather,' Jeremy suggested as he sank down on one of the small, blue dining chairs next to a small, round blue dining table. Blanche and Back Shed did the same. Leaning his elbows on the table, Jeremy looked exhausted. 'This is turning into a nightmare,' he whimpered.

'Well it's too late to stop now. Anyway, all we have to do is to grab the duffel coat, get Blanche to try it on and then we can go.' Back Shed was determined to rally his troops again. 'In fact, I'm sure that we can manage without you if you want to go outside and sit with Sandy. He must be getting a bit fed up sitting on that wall on his own.'

'No, no, what about the toggle fastenings? You might want help with those. We really need little Treasure, but I'm not sure we will be able to persuade her to come out of that pram.' Jeremy indicated the pram with his head.

'We'll see about that.' Blanche went and stood over the pram. She could just see one of Little Treasure's back paws sticking out from under the pillow. 'Come on, it's time for you to do your bit.' The pillow moved and Little Treasure popped her head out. At first, Blanche didn't recognise her. She was wearing a white hat with a frill around the edge. 'What on earth are you wearing and where did you get it?'

'I was really, really terrified and shaking because I thought the bear was going to attack me. Then, I saw this pram and it seemed like a good place to hide. Then I found this hat under this pillow and when I put it on, it made me feel better. It's lovely and I want it so much.'

'There's nowhere for your ears to go, they're all flattened down.' Blanche's voice was beginning to sound painfully hoarse. 'Plus, it isn't very Bollywood, is it?'

'I don't care, I want it, I want it.' Blanche blew through her nose. This was blackmail; it was clear that Little Treasure was not going to help unless she let her keep the hat and Blanche didn't have the energy to argue.

'Oh alright, but you can't wear it all the time, your ears will go all droopy like one of those floppy-eared rabbits. Now, get a wriggle on, the bear is only a toy and you press a button to make its head and legs work. Back Shed has found the button and switched it off.'

Little Treasure pushed the hat frill back and pulled her ears up straight. Then she peered over the edge of the pram and checked to see if the bear really had stopped moving. When she saw that it was still lying where she had left it, she decided it was safe to leave her hiding place.

She hopped out of the pram and went over to look at the toggles on the duffel coat. Back Shed had turned the bear over so he was lying on the floor looking up at them and Little Treasure was able to examine each one closely. Getting so close to the bear was a bit worrying because he still had a very knowing expression on his face. Taking her courage in both paws she bent down to see what was what. With a grunt of satisfaction, she saw that only one toggle was fastened and that one hadn't done up properly. Stealing herself, she clamped her teeth around it and yanked at the toggle. Suddenly, the coat was gaping open.

'Hurrah, hurrah!' they all cried loudly. Their cry was so loud that Sandy heard them and he smiled; things must be going to plan.

Back Shed levered the bear to his feet. Nodding at Blanche, he grabbed one side of the coat in his teeth and Blanche grabbed the other then they slowly backed away from the bear. But Back Shed was a bit too eager and his ample bottom bumped into a farmyard display, knocking all the wooden animals flying. Quickly picking up a broom, with a picture of Cinderella on it, Jeremy called. 'Leave it, leave it, I'll brush these animals out of your way. It could be painful if you step on one.'

'Thanks.' Back Shed and Blanche carried on pulling at the coat. Then it happened. Without warning, the coat slid down the bear's short arms and off his body. Surprised that it had been so easy, Blanche and Back Shed were left holding the shoulders of the coat between their teeth. Delighted, they dropped them and Back Shed grabbed Blanche and waltzed her around the blue dining table.

Not everyone was so happy. The bear glowered at them defiantly; he definitely gave the impression that he was feeling very bitter about what was going on. After all, a gang of hooligan cats had removed his coat and was obviously going to steal it. He would be left looking ridiculous just wearing his floppy hat and wellies Back Shed sensed how the bear was feeling and apologised. 'Sorry matey, we need the coat more than you do.' Without saying a word, the bear made it plain that he did not believe him, but Back Shed couldn't stop to explain, he had to get on. What was he doing anyway, trying to smooth things over with a mechanical, toy bear?

The next challenge was to see if they could get the coat on Blanche. Once again, Little Treasure would be needed to sort out any toggle problems that might crop up. But she was not paying attention any longer; she was too busy admiring her hat in a Snow White hand-mirror. She was thrilled with the way the frill framed her face. 'Stop playing with that mirror, give us a hand, or a paw, if it's not too much trouble,' Jeremy quipped. However,

Little Treasure, was far too absorbed with her reflection to pay attention to Jeremy's sarcasm.

Eventually, she remembered what she was supposed to be doing and tore herself away from the mirror. 'Coming,' she sang out and joined Back Shed and Jeremy as they tried to fit the coat on Blanche. It proved to be trickier than they expected. Blanche stood up and held out her front paws straight in front of her. Concentrating as hard as they could, Back Shed and Jeremy pushed the sleeves on them. Of course, that didn't work because they ought to have realised that it should have been one sleeve first, the, the coat had to go round the back of Blanche so they could put on the other sleeve. As it was, the coat was hanging down between Blanche's front paws.

Silently, they looked at it; nobody was going to admit that they had been so stupid.

Catching sight of the bear out of the corner of his eye, Back Shed thought he saw it sneering, but told himself he must be imagining it. Giving himself a shake, he helped Jeremy pull the coat off Blanche. They tried again with more success this time and, after a few minutes, Blanche stood before them actually wearing the blue duffel coat.

'What do you think?' her voice still sounded a bit husky. She wasn't sure if it was right size because it only reached just below her waist. It had seemed bigger when the bear was wearing it.

'It works, it works!' shouted Back Shed triumphantly. 'It could have been made for you.' Blanche was pleased but a little self-conscious and she felt herself blushing.

Turning around so they could see the back, she made herself as tall and erect as she could. 'Is it too short, is it okay? It looked longer on the bear. Don't say it's okay if you don't mean it.'

'Trust me, Blanchey Baby, it really could have been made for you,' gushed back Shed. 'It looks great and I don't think we have to bother fastening the toggles at this stage. You look fabulous; would I lie to you, would I?'

Not wanting to cause trouble by mentioning all the lies he

had actually told her in the past, Blanche felt that it was best not to answer him. 'Well, that's it then, it looks as if I'll be going to university with Lucy after all.'

Feeling a sense of real achievement, they started to congratulate each other. But Jeremy brought them back down to earth when he asked impatiently, 'Can we go home now? All this stress has taken years off my life.' To be fair, he did appear to have developed frown lines on his forehead since they had left the Close earlier. Now that they had got what they had come for and he was making no secret of the fact that he thought that they should leave as soon as possible.

'Right men, mission accomplished, are we ready to go?' Back Shed squared his shoulders. 'Are we ready to go, men?' he repeated.

'I'm not a man, am I Mum?' Little Treasure chirped. With tight lips, Blanche just thrust her forcefully toward the back of the shop and the toilet window without answering.

Before he followed the others, Back Shed manoeuvred the bear through the front flap of a green wigwam near the doll's pram. It didn't feel right to leave him, in the middle of the shop, without his coat. As he made his way to the toilet window, he could have sworn he heard the words, 'I'll get you for this!'; his imagination was really beginning to get the better of him.

When they had all made a safe getaway from the shop they re-joined Sandy. He was still sitting on the litter bin and had started to doze. 'You could be court-marshalled for sleeping on duty,' barked Back Shed.

Ignoring Back Shed, Sandy stretched and yawned. That looks nice he said, indicating the duffel coat Blanche was wearing. 'Are we going home now?'

'Yes, yes we are.' Jeremy was already making his way from the front of the shop into the High Street.

'Hold on, I need to tell you something Back Shed announced. I'm not going to come all the way to the Close with you. If I turn off into that narrow alley near the middle of the High Street,

I'm almost home.' Spluttering, he hurriedly corrected himself. 'I don't mean a real home. I mean I can find a place to sleep for the night around there. Can you find your way back if I go off and find a place to lay my head?' he asked hopefully. He was actually tired out and wanted his own, comfortable bed in his posh house but there was no way he was going to admit that, was he?

'Whatever,' Jeremy sighed. He was pretty sure that they could find their own way back easily enough and he just wanted to get going. They began their return journey up the High Street. The shops were still as fascinating as they had been earlier. It was a real shame that they couldn't do any exploring but Jeremy had made it clear that he wanted to crack on. When Back Shed's turn-off came up, he gave them an exaggerated salute. 'See you all soon,' he called. Playfully, he flung the duffel coat hood over Blanche's head and humming loudly he strolled away feeling very pleased with himself. In the morning, he would dash to the Close as soon as he woke up and had had something to eat. He couldn't wait to tell all the cats from the Close and The Avenue how brilliant he had been in his latest and perhaps greatest adventure.

Blanche, Jeremy, Sandy and Little Treasure continued up the High Street. When they reached the Market Square. Blanche and Sandy shot a look at each other. The shop that had driven Little Treasure wild was just ahead. The one with all the sparkling rings, necklaces and bracelets. Luckily, Little Treasure was still wearing her white hat and Blanche made a snap decision. Quick as a flash, she shook off the hood of the duffel coat and pulled the white hat down over Little Treasure's eyes, hurriedly dragging her past the shop. The duffel coat was a bit hot and the sleeves restricted her front paw movements but she managed to propel Little Treasure as far as the Cathedral Green. 'What are you doing? I can't see anything,' Little Treasure protested.

'Just as well and you aren't going to see anything when we get to the traffic lights either. We can't be doing with any more of your malarkey.'

Lifting up the hat frill, Little Treasure gave Blanche a winning smile. 'Well, can I pull the hat down over my eyes myself, you are too rough?' Secretly, she thought she would still be able to see the lights if she didn't pull the hat down all the way.

'Dream on,' Blanche was not fooled for a minute and when the traffic lights loomed ahead, she jammed the hat down so firmly that it covered her daughter's nose as well as her eyes. Little Treasure thought her mother was being very harsh because, not only was she temporarily blinded, she couldn't breathe properly either. But what could she do? Blanche was her mother and stronger than she was.

After the cats crossed over at the traffic lights toward Saint Thomas Street, Blanche lifted the hat so that Little Treasure could see again. It was still quiet as they started up the deserted street. Although they wanted to get home as soon as they could, they were all aware that they might never come this way again. It was a moment to remember and even Jeremy slowed his pace a little. When they passed the wooden soldier they even took the time to study his face. With his painted, twirly moustache and painted, rosy cheeks, he didn't seem as scary any more. Leaving him behind and with many backward glances at the way they had come, they finally arrived at the Close. Looking at their tired faces, Blanche felt guilty because everyone had done so much for her that night but she still needed one more favour from Jeremy and Sandy.

'Will you help me to take off this coat? I'm not going to let Lucy see it yet; it's going to be a surprise. I'll hide it under the rest of her university things until the last minute. She will be so impressed when she sees that I am all prepared for our new life together.' Dutifully, Jeremy gave instructions to Sandy and they worked the coat off Blanche and pulled it free from her front paws. Holding the coat between her teeth, Blanche could only mumble, 'Thanks for everything, I won't forget how much I owe you.'

'It's been quite exciting,' Sandy grinned.

'Humph, you didn't have to do anything,' Jeremy sounded

very resentful as he made for their house. Shrugging his shoulders, Sandy followed him. Blanche and Little Treasure watched until they disappeared from sight. Turning toward their own house, they managed to tug the coat over the garden wall and push it through the broken cat flap. Soundlessly, they pulled it up the stairs and into the spare room. Pushing the big red bean bag aside, they hid it at the bottom of Lucy's university pile.

Looking very pleased with herself Little Treasure looked at Blanche with an expectant expression. 'Was I good tonight, Mum?' Blanche was lost for words and gawped at her. Was it really possible that she had no idea how much trouble she had actually caused?

'Yes, yes,' she lied, 'just go to bed.' There didn't seem to be any point telling her what a pain she had been. Happily, Little Treasure tripped back downstairs and jumped up onto the surface and into her basket in the utility room. Blanche shook her head from side to side. 'Where did I go wrong?' she mumbled. She gave herself a shake and went into Lucy's room. Softly, she crept onto the bed and snuggled up beside her under the duvet. Laying her head next to Lucy's on the pillow, she closed her eyes and fell fast asleep for the rest of the night.

CHAPTER 13

The Departure

The next morning, Blanche woke herself up by snoring loudly but Lucy didn't budge; she was obviously not ready to leave the moon world and come into the world of light. Still feeling the effects of the night before, she slowly crawled out of bed without disturbing her. She made her way downstairs and had a quick drink before going out into the garden for a widdle. When she came back into the house she realised how late it was. Andrew had already left for work and Clare was in the shower. Rubbing her eyes, she stumbled through the lounge to take up her official position on the windowsill.

She was soon jerked wide awake by the unexpected sight before her. Some sort of meeting was taking place outside the front of Jeremy and Sandy's house. She could even hear someone speaking to the crowd. All the cats belonging to the CAALE seemed to be present, plus some other cats she didn't recognise. What on earth did they think they were doing? They couldn't call a meeting without the consent of the Chaircat and she was the Chaircat. Was this an unauthorised takeover? Scrambling through the open window, she marched over intending to confront the ringleaders.

When she reached the crowd of cats, they parted to let her through to the front. Now she could see who was speaking. She should have known, there was only one cat that could draw a crowd as large as this. Of course, it was none other than Back Shed. He was standing on top of a dark grey cat carrier. Jeremy and Sandy's people had forgotten to take the carrier out of the car after they had taken Jeremy to the vet for his injections a few days ago. They had cleared the car out that morning because they were going away for the day and had hurriedly dumped the carrier on the front path.

This was a stroke of luck for Back Shed. When he saw it, he had rubbed his front paws together and smiled with satisfaction. Using the carrier as a platform would give him a lofty position. It would make him look very important and everyone would be able to see him. Huffing and puffing, he had scrabbled on top of it. From his elevated position, he had called the crowd together. Now, he was enthralling his audience, holding everyone spellbound with vivid descriptions of his daring toy shop exploits of the night before. Using dramatic gestures, he was portraying himself as a feline superhero yet again.

Sounds of 'Ooh!' and 'Ahh!' were heard. Some of the cats were even clapping. The bits of his breakfast that were stuck to his chin didn't seem to detract from what he was saying. Suddenly, his voice became unsure and died away; he had caught sight of Blanche and she did not look happy. Quickly recovering himself, Back Shed jumped off the cat carrier and threw his front paws around her in a suffocating hug. 'Blanchey Baby!'

'Let me go,' Blanche yelled at him. There was no doubt that her voice had returned to its full strength. She struggled free and tugged her fur back into place. Looking around at all the eager faces, she could see that they were excited about Back Shed's tales of 'daring do'. But they were also bewildered because he had let them know that Blanche was leaving the Close soon. Apart from the fact that he had broken his promise not to tell anyone, this momentous information had been nothing less than a bombshell to the local cats and their excitement was mixed with uncertainty. They obviously expected her to reassure them and say that it wasn't true; but this wasn't to be.

She looked at the eager faces around her. Surely now was the time that she should let them know what was going on. It also seemed the right time to make her farewell speech to her loyal supporters. With a sinking feeling in her heart, she climbed onto the cat carrier and took a deep breath. 'Last night, Back Shed, Jeremy, Sandy, Little Treasure and myself had to perform a dangerous operation. We had to go down into the High Street, break into a toy shop and take something that did not belong to us. We had to face many risks but we got back safely. The operation was necessary and I'm sure that Back Shed has told you why. But don't think, for a moment, that I approve of what we did. Don't think that I expect any of you to copy us. It was reckless and we could have been injured or killed. Do you understand?' She fixed a steely glare on every cat in turn.

'Yes,' they shouted with one voice. Of course, Back Shed didn't join in; he had to keep up his reputation of being the cat who made his own rules.

'Finally, I would like to say that I am sorry to be leaving the Close. I have enjoyed my time as Chaircat of the CAALE and I have always been grateful for your support and loyalty.' Some of the cats started to raise their front paws because they wanted to ask questions. There was so much they needed to know.

Blanche pointed at The Wise White Cat at the front of the crowd and waited for him to speak first. In a deep voice he asked, 'Dear friend and leader, when are you going away?'

'Yes, when, when, when?' the crowd repeated. Holding her paw up for silence, Blanche told them that she did not know the exact date, but the day for her departure could be very soon. Some of the cats looked extremely shaken. Many of the older ones even started to cry quietly.

'Perhaps we should ask the rest of our questions when we have all had a more time to pull ourselves together?' The Wise White Cat suggested. 'We can all meet again tomorrow.'

There was general agreement and the crowd began to break up. Most of the cats surrounded Blanche as she walked back to her house. They just wanted to touch her on the shoulder or clasp her front paws. Never missing the opportunity to be the centre of attention, Little Treasure suddenly appeared beside her mother. She could see that Blanche was upset, but that didn't stop her showing off. 'Come on, Mum, I'll take you home now.' She made sure that everyone could hear her being so thoughtful.

Now they would all know that she could be a caring daughter as well a beautiful one.

Blanche wasn't fooled for a minute. 'We are home,' she muttered under her breath and gave Little Treasure a withering look. Undaunted, Little Treasure followed her as she jumped into their house through the lounge window. As soon as she was out of sight of the crowd, Little Treasure rushed to her basket and pulled her new white hat out from under her princess duvet. Then, she went off to admire herself in the bathroom mirror. 'So much for the caring daughter performance,' Blanche sniffed dismissively.

Springing back on the windowsill, Blanche looked to see if any of the cats had seen Little Treasure's speedy getaway. But they had formed small groups and were probably discussing who would be the next Chaircat of the Association. No doubt Back Shed fancied himself as the main contender. Of course, he was not even a resident, let alone a member, but that wouldn't stop him. He might even try to move into the Close if he could find a gullible family to adopt him. She hoped it wouldn't be her family.

Blanche pressed her front paw against her forehead. She was so mixed up. She couldn't work out how she felt about everything. She was thankful that Back Shed had helped her to get the duffel coat, but she resented him because she suspected that his motive had something to do with an ambition was to replace her as Chaircat.

On top of that, she was really sad that she was leaving, even though she was happy that she was going to be with Lucy. To make things worse, she became nervous every time she thought about her future at a university. How could she have all these feelings at the same time? How could she make sense of them? She gave a shuddering sigh and decided to go and sit by the pond in the back garden. She wanted to work things out and the pleasant sound of the fountain always calmed her down.

Before she settled down by the pond, she stopped to watch Helena and Georgio warming up for their session in the greenhouse again. Was it only yesterday that she was sitting here watching them doing exactly the same thing? So much had happened since then but it seemed like an age ago.

This morning, Helena was sitting on her plant pot, rolling her shoulders back and forth. Georgio was propped up against the greenhouse door, flexing his back legs. 'How'sa theengs,' he called, 'dida hyou manage to geta duffela coat and pena thing sorted out?' He started flexing his front legs.

Blanche nodded, she wasn't sure if he and Helena knew the full story of the trip to the toyshop, but she wasn't really in the mood to fill them in. Anyway, Back Shed would tell them his version soon enough. She supposed that she should let them know that she was leaving soon. It probably wouldn't make much difference to them; they didn't get involved in the cat politics of the Close. However, when Blanche strolled over to let them know that she would be moving away, she was surprised at their reaction; they were visibly upset. 'Do you mean we will have to ask Little Treasure if we need to know something?' Helena asked. She looked at Georgio and they stared at each other in horror. 'Oh no!' they gasped together. It was quite obvious that they were not relishing the prospect of dealing with Little Treasure instead of her mother, but it could happen. After all, she was Blanche's daughter. If the CAALE didn't replace Blanche straight away, it was possible that Little Treasure would become the acting Chaircat until they voted in the new one.

Of course, this was going to cause problems. Not just for the members but also for all residents of the Close who Blanche had helped and advised over the years. For a start, you could never get a straight answer from Little Treasure and she was always looking for compliments. She also wasted so much time talking about things that didn't matter and Georgio couldn't afford to waste time. He was going to hibernate soon and he had a deadline to keep. However, the worst thing for them was that Little Treasure didn't know anything about iPads, online or Andrew's Credit Card. While they were struggling to take all this in, Little Treasure pranced out of the broken cat flap in the back door.

She was wearing her frilly, white hat and dragging a red and gold tassel behind her. 'Hi! I've got one, I've got one. I've just chewed this off the silk cushion in Clare and Andrew's bedroom. There are three left and I'll get another one later. What do you think, does it go with my hat?' She gave them a dazzling smile.

'Don't you think there are more important things to think about?' Helena asked disapprovingly.

'I know my hat isn't really a Bollywood look but I could hang the tassel from it. Do you think it will work?'

'It will look gorgeous sweetie.' They hadn't noticed Back Shed quietly watching them from the garage roof.

'Unbelievable,' Helena glared up at him, Back Shed obviously wasn't picking up on the tense atmosphere; he just shrugged and grinned down at her. With a sharp intake of breath, Helena slithered up to Little Treasure and banged a tiny hand on her front paw. 'I wasn't talking about your hat or your stupid tassel. I was talking about your mother going away. For one thing, have you thought about who is going to take care of you?'

Jerking his head vigorously, Georgio repeated the question adding, 'Hyou dona knowa how lucky hyou are. Before hwe cama to thees garden, some of us hada to maka our owna way in the world, we hada noa friends, noa family. Perhaps isa time hyou standa hon hyour owna paws.' His accent sounded more pronounced when he was annoyed.

Little Treasure's mouth fell open. 'What are you talking about? My mum will find a way to sort things out, won't you, Mum?' She looked at Blanche, but Blanche avoided her eyes and didn't say anything. The seriousness of the situation began to dawn on Little Treasure for the first time. Her mother, the only cat who was always there for her no matter what she said or did, was really leaving her and going to a faraway place.

She knew that Blanche had been going on about Lucy, university and leaving but she never thought it would happen.

Even when they stole the duffel coat from the bear, she didn't think it would lead to this. She whimpered softly as she sank down on the grass, brushing away her red and gold tassel, as it fell beside her.

An uncomfortable silence fell over the garden. The only sounds came from Little Treasure's soft sobs and the gentle splash of the fountain. Even Back Shed was lost for words. Then, as if by magic, The Wise White Cat appeared on the garage roof beside Back Shed. Jumping down, he went to sit by Little Treasure. 'I couldn't help overhearing what you have all been saying. I know it was a private conversation, but do you mind if I make a contribution?' He looked at Blanche; she cleared her throat and told him to go ahead.

'There is another way to think about this,' he said kindly, placing one of his front paws on the top of Little Treasure's head. 'It's true that things are going to change.' He paused, 'And when those changes have taken place, Clare and Andrew will be lonely and sad. The question is, who will they turn to? Who will be the centre of their attention? Who will be the only one left in the house for them to care for and love?'

Little Treasure began to blink quickly as pictures of herself being petted and pampered flashed through her head. Oh yes, she could get used to that. She straightened up; all of a sudden, her future looked brighter. 'I think I'll be alright, Mum, I'm going to be brave because I know you have to go wherever Lucy goes. You mustn't worry about me.' Dramatically throwing back her shoulders, she picked up her tassel and walked back to the house doing her best to look like she was sacrificing her own happiness for her mother's. It nearly worked, but the illusion was spoiled because she started talking to herself when she thought she was out of earshot. She could be heard working out how she was going to impress Clare and Andrew when she wore her tassels and did her latest Bollywood act for them.

Blanche gave wry smile and thanked The Wise White Cat. With great dignity, he bowed his head. 'There is one more thing you ought to know, my friend. I have just received a message from The Great Cat God of Destiny. The message instructed me to reveal that Lucy will be going away very soon so I think you should prepare yourself for the departure.' Again, he bowed his head. 'I will leave you now.' Blanche saluted him and he leapt back onto the garage roof. Back Shed respectfully moved to let him pass, but as he did so, Back Shed accidentally made a horrible bottom smell. Startled, The Wise White Cat swung round and sniffed. Satisfied that the smell had not come from his own bottom this time, he gave Back Shed a dirty look and swiftly disappeared from view. Back Shed refused to be embarrassed. Guffawing, he made another horrible, bottom smell and then pointed his bottom at Helena and Georgio and waggled it in air. He could be so uncouth.

Helena and Georgio didn't want to encourage his vulgar behaviour so they just shook their heads and returned to the greenhouse to continue their session. They wouldn't play any music today; it didn't seem appropriate somehow. Blanche didn't even bother telling Back Shed not to be such a prat. Why should she? He wouldn't get the respect he needed to be a member of the CAALE, let alone Chaircat, if he kept acting like a yobo and that suited her. With a superior smile on her face, she strolled over to the pond and stretched out, she would try to sleep. Who knows, she might not have many more opportunities to enjoy the tranquillity of this special place?

Later, she was grateful that she did manage to get some sleep that day because she didn't get any that night. How could she sleep when the air was suddenly crackling with so much nervous expectation? Clare and Andrew were restless and agitated. Blanche could hear them moving about and talking softly in their bedroom. Clare even went down to the kitchen to make a cup of tea in the early hours of the morning. Lucy didn't bother trying to sleep and watched her TV for most of the night. Eventually, Blanche managed to drift off but Clare came to wake Lucy a short time later. 'It's time to get up Lu. Dad's already packing the car.' Lucy sat up and yawned. She gave Blanche a hug and looked as if she was going to cry. Something wasn't right.

Blanche could see Andrew passing Lucy's bedroom, carrying things downstairs. It took her a few minutes to realise that he was carrying things from Lucy's university pile to the car. She felt her stomach churning, this must be it. This must be the day they were leaving. Her mind raced, she would not have time to do all the things she had planned. She wouldn't even have time to organise her official resignation from the CAALE and propose a new Chaircat and what about saying goodbye to her closest friends?

She tried not to panic, she had to stay calm and think what to do first. She would need to get her duffel coat from the bottom of the university pile. Gently, pulling away from Lucy she slid down from the bed. Waiting until Andrew was outside packing the car, she crept into the spare room and dug out her duffel coat. She chuckled to herself; Lucy would be so thrilled and surprised when she saw her Blanche wearing it. Of course, she must remember to get a pen as well.

She stuffed the coat behind the spare bedroom door and then saw Andrew's jacket hanging over the banisters at the top of the stairs; a small pen was poking out of the top pocket. She pulled the pen out with her teeth, rolled it down the stairs and out of the open front door; she would leave it there for the moment. Now for the coat, she would need help to put it on. But, before she decided who to ask, she heard a shuffling sound outside. Jeremy and Sandy had come over. Blanche stepped out of the front door to join them. 'What are you doing here?'

'Early this morning, The Wise White Cat came and told us that Lucy would be leaving today.' As usual, Jeremy looked worried.

Keeping his voice as low pitched as he could, Sandy added, 'He's told all the other cats too. How does he know such things?'

'He has the power to communicate with The Great Cat God of Destiny.' Blanche paused thoughtfully, 'Truly, he is the most remarkable member of our Association.' Shaking her head, she turned her mind back to what she needed to do next. 'Anyway, now you're here will you help me to put my coat on? I was going to ask Little Treasure, but I could end up wearing it upside down.'

'Of course we will,' they answered, 'but where is it?'

'It's upstairs in the spare room,' Blanche managed to blurt out as she was pushed aside by Andrew as he came back through the front door.

'Out of the way boys,' Andrew instructed breathlessly, nearly falling over Jeremy and Sandy, as he rushed toward the stairs for more of Lucy's stuff.

'Come on, let's get out of the way.' Blanche beckoned them to follow her across the drive to the garage. She stopped just inside the open garage door. 'You stay here, I'll go and get my coat. Then, when I am all dressed up in it, I can pick up my pen; I left it by the front door. When I have got my pen, I think it would be best if I just came back here and waited with you until it's time to go. I can see everything that's happening from here.' A mischievous gleam appeared in her eyes. 'When the car is packed, I will suddenly appear and surprise Lucy.' Blanche paused, 'Yes, I think that's probably the best way to play it, Lucy won't be expecting anything like this.'

Jeremy and Sandy looked at each other. 'Are you sure you shouldn't just check to see if everything is going to plan?' Jeremy asked.

'No, no, it's all fine.' Blanche paused again. Then, she gave a decisive sigh, 'Right! Got to get on, no time to lose. I'd better go and get my coat from the spare room now.'

As she briskly padded back into the house, she became aware that many pairs of eyes were watching her. She was taken aback and touched to see that there were cats everywhere. They were sitting on garden paths, in doorways and on roofs. Some of the younger ones were sitting on the branches of trees. A few were passing the time by trying to do gymnastics. They were twisting their bodies round and round the lower branches. One youthful tabby was quite good, tumbling and swinging over and under his branch. Blanche nearly yelled at him to take it easy because he would make himself dizzy, but she didn't. She didn't have the heart to throw her weight about today.

Of course, Back Shed had turned up, but he wasn't going join the other cats and watch from a distance. He was going to get as close to the action and to Blanche's house as possible. Spotting Jeremy and Sandy in Blanche's garage, he sauntered over to join them. Of course, he had quickly worked out that it was obviously the best place to see what was happening because it was as near to the house and the car as he could get.

By the time Little Treasure finally appeared on the scene most of the cats had already settled down to wait for Blanche's final farewell. Catching sight of Little Treasure, they were startled to see that she wasn't looking her best. She had obviously got up in a hurry, she hadn't smoothed down her fur and she hadn't put on her new hat. She wasn't even carrying a tassel. Perhaps she sensed that something momentous was happening and panicked.

But when she arrived at the front door and saw how many cats there were in the Close, she was genuinely flabbergasted. What was happening? Why had they all turned up at once? It was a bit of a mystery but then a light switched on in her tiny mind and a brilliant idea came to her. It didn't matter why they were there, surely this was an opportunity not to be missed. Looking at all the cats sitting and waiting she thought: AUDIENCE.

Smoothing her fur into place as she rushed back to her basket for her hat and tassel, she planned her performance. This was it; this was her chance to become a star. Arriving back at the front door she danced out onto the lawn and grabbed a dandelion stalk. Holding the stalk up, and using the flower like a microphone, she called out, 'Would you like me to dance and sing some Bollywood songs while you are waiting?'

The cats, who were close enough to hear her, shifted uncomfortably and looked away. Little Treasure was taken aback. Why were they so quiet? Why weren't they cheering her on? Leaving his position under the chestnut tree, The Wise White Cat came to her rescue. He took one of her paws in his and said gently, 'We will all hear your songs another day. Now is not the time for singing.'

Clearly feeling put out she retorted, 'Suit yourselves, you don't know what you're missing.' Tossing her head in the air, she stalked over to Jeremy, Sandy and Back Shed waiting in the garage. Who knows, the others might start to change their minds if they ended up hanging around for longer than they expected?

She sat down next to Jeremy and asked him if he knew what was going on. He swallowed a few times and tried not to make eye-contact, 'I think you ought to know that your mother is leaving in a short while.'

'What, today, now?' Little Treasure tried to make sense of what he had said. She swallowed and struggled to speak. 'It's a bit short notice, isn't it?'

'Hmm, it is,' Jeremy agreed. 'It's caused quite a bit of confusion, but The Wise White Cat has let everyone know that Lucy is leaving today and we are all here to say goodbye.'

'He didn't let me know, I should have been the first cat he told. After all, I am the cat who is losing her mother.' Jeremy didn't know what to say, so he didn't say anything. He just started to lick the fur on his neck and shoulders. He didn't want to get involved in a scene with Little Treasure; it wasn't the right time. She could be quite aggressive when she thought she had been side-lined plus, arguing with her might make him miss something important.

In a huff she got up and sidled over to Back Shed. Breathing hard, she stared at him, hoping for some kind of support. Back Shed took no notice of her and started to hum quietly. Little Treasure thought about swiping him over the ear, but as she was about to strike, another brilliant idea came to her. Maybe Back Shed would do a duet with her. They could do a little farewell concert for her mother, with a special goodbye song. She had heard someone singing something about doing things their way on the radio the other day. It wasn't Bollywood music but they could sing the words to a Bollywood tune. It would be 'Easy Peasy Lemon Squeezy!'

Before she had time to ask Back Shed about doing a duet, her mother almost fell into the garage. She was stumbling over the duffel coat as she bundled it in after her. 'The back door is open so I came that way, I don't want Lucy to see my coat yet, it will spoil the surprise,' she panted. 'Will you help me to put it on now?' Jeremy, Sandy and Back Shed all sprang to her side; they couldn't do enough for her. After all, this was her last day in the Close. Tugging and pulling until the coat fitted as perfectly as they could make it, they stood back to admire their handiwork.

'Thank you, thank you, I know I have said this before, but I really don't know what I would have done without your help. I'm really sorry that I will not have time to say an individual goodbye to everyone, I haven't even managed to say a proper goodbye to Helena and Georgio. Little Treasure will have to say goodbye to them for me.' Pausing for a moment, she added, 'I do have time to say goodbye to you though.' Blanche felt a lump forming in her throat and she could hardly speak. 'Goodbye my true friends,' she whispered haltingly. Afraid she was going to break down, she coughed to cover her embarrassment and only managed to stutter, 'I will miss you so much.'

She sat down by Little Treasure and gently stroked her. Little Treasure buried her head in her mother's shoulder fur and started to cry. She didn't feel like singing anymore. She hiccuped and whimpered, 'I want my piece of blue velvet.'

Seeing that Andrew had stopped putting things in the car, Sandy gently touched Blanche on the shoulder, 'I think it's time to go.' For the first time in his life, his voice sounded quite deep. 'I think the car is all packed.'

'Thank you again,' rubbing heads with Jeremy, Sandy and Back Shed, Blanche shakily walked out of the garage with Little Treasure following close behind her. Trying to be helpful, Little Treasure found Blanche's pen by the front door and started rolling it to the car using her nose. She only stopped when she bumped into one of the car tyres and got some dirt on her paws.

Andrew was standing by the driver's door. It was open and he was sorting out some keys. Blanche wasn't sure where she would be sitting, so she parked herself by one of the doors at the rear of the car. Little Treasure pushed the pen forward and flopped down beside her. Clare and Lucy were nowhere to be seen.

Andrew started jiggling the keys. 'Time to go,' he called in the direction of the house, 'we don't want to get caught up in the traffic.' Jeremy thought he sounded stressed and a bit impatient.

Lucy came out of the front door first. Her eyes were very red and she kept dabbing them with a tissue. By the time Clare appeared Lucy was getting in the front passenger seat. Blanche wondered what was happening. Why hadn't Lucy showed her where her seat was? She could see that the car was full of university stuff, but she could easily squeeze in somewhere. When she stopped wiping her eyes with the tissue, perhaps Lucy would make room for her in the front. That would be the very first time she would be able to see her wearing the duffel coat and holding the pen. Blanche felt like hugging herself as she pictured Lucy cheering up and laughing with delight.

Blanche hoped that her duffel coat and pen would cheer Clare up too. She was crying loudly and bending over to hug Lucy. It wasn't easy to make out what she was saying. It sounded like, 'Stay safe, eat properly and phone me when you get there.' Andrew pulled Lucy and Clare apart. Wiping the tears away from Clare's eyes with his hand, he told her to go back into the house, but she wasn't listening. She just kept staring at Lucy.

'When are you going to get in the car, Mum?' On this occasion, Little Treasure wasn't the only one who didn't understand what was happening. 'Don't forget your pen.'

'I'll go and stand outside Lucy's door so she can see me through the window. You follow me with the pen.' Straightening her coat with her front paws, she moved quickly and looked up at Lucy expectantly. But Lucy still had a tissue pressed to her face. As

she tried to attract her attention, Blanche could hear the cats cheering her and she turned to wave at them. All of a sudden, without warning, the car's engine was switched on. Blanche and Little Treasure leapt back in surprise and watched helplessly as the car moved forward and slowly swung out of the drive.

Blanche tried to shout over the noise as the car moved out onto the Close but it was impossible, it was too loud. She waved frantically as it speeded up and disappeared around the corner, into The Avenue and out of sight. Surely this wasn't meant to happen. Surely, the car wasn't supposed to take Lucy away to university without her. A stunned silence fell over the scene. Only the muffled sound of Clare's sobbing could be heard as she rushed back indoors the minute the car had was driven out of sight into The Avenue. Blanche just sat on the drive in a daze, she couldn't move. Lucy was gone, she couldn't believe it; Lucy had left her behind and she hadn't even seen her duffel coat and pen.

As the minutes ticked away, Blanche's heart told her that Lucy and Andrew wouldn't be coming back for her, but she stayed on the drive anyway. She tried to convince herself that the car was going to reappear. It would screech to a stop when they saw her. Lucy would leap out, scoop her up in her arms and they would set off for their new life together. She strained her eyes and ears for any sound or sight of the car returning. She waited and waited for a very, very long time, but the car didn't come.

The other cats who had come to see her off didn't know what to do to help. They could see that Blanche was heart-broken so they waited with her. They just wanted to be there if she needed them for anything. But Blanche didn't move or say a single word; she just sat and stared out toward The Avenue. Eventually, as the sun began to drop out of sight, they quietly started to drift away. All except The Wise White Cat.

After he had told Little Treasure to save her singing for another day, he chose to distance himself and sit apart from the others. He couldn't bear to be too close to the suffering he had helped to cause. He shook his wise head from side to side while asking himself the same question over and over again. Why hadn't he let Blanche know that The Great Cat God of Destiny had only revealed that Lucy was leaving the Close? Why hadn't he let Blanche know that she had not been present in the leaving vision? But deep down, he knew the answer. He was too weak. He just couldn't bear to see the agony in her eyes as she began to understand the significance of his meaning. Today, he had failed in his duty to her and today he must confess his weakness to his God and beg for forgiveness.

The Wise White Cat cut a forlorn figure in the darkening Close. He sat rooted to the spot watching Jeremy, Sandy and Back Shed as they tried to get Blanche to leave the drive, but she wouldn't move. 'Shall I pinch her?' Little Treasure whispered. 'It might make her get up.'

'I don't think that would be a good idea,' Sandy answered as he signalled to Jeremy and Back Shed to help him to get rid of the duffel coat. They took it off Blanche as quickly and as gently as they could and stuffed it behind a bag of cement in the garage. Blanche didn't try to stop them. But they left the pen where it was; one of the people from the Close would find it and pick it up later.

'Come on, Blanchey Baby, time to go inside,' Back Shed propelled her soothingly but firmly down the path at the side of the house, toward the cat flap in the back door. Jeremy pushed open the bottom of the cat flap carefully because it was only hanging on by one screw after it had got broken the night before. Sandy and Back Shed tenderly nudged her through.

'Take care of her,' Jeremy whispered to Little Treasure as she slipped into the house behind her mother.

Walking away Jeremy and Sandy were outraged when Back Shed mumbled, 'I don't suppose there will be a vacancy for Chaircat now.' He really was incredibly insensitive. How could he think of saying such a thing at a time like this?

Once she was inside the house, Blanche stumbled up the stairs to Lucy's bedroom. Little Treasure thought her mother looked older somehow and she followed her to make sure she didn't fall. Blanche managed to reach the top of the stairs but she struggled as she jumped onto Lucy's bed. All she wanted to do was to bury herself under the duvet and never come out again. Little Treasure watched as her mother gave a long, shuddering sigh and crawled down into the bed where nobody could see her. She felt very lost and upset so she went and fetched her piece of blue velvet then stretched out on the rug beside the bed.

One of Lucy's teddy bears had fallen on the floor and she rested her head on its body. She knew she wasn't the brightest cat in the Close, but even she was capable of working out that this had been the worst day in Blanche's life. Fretfully, Little Treasure wondered if her mother would ever be the same again. Would she ever recover and be the cat everyone had always loved and respected?

Epilogue

After Lucy had left, Clare wandered aimlessly around the house for hours. She could not go into Lucy's bedroom without breaking down; it seemed so empty without her. But she had to wash the sheets and duvet cover sometime, so she may as well get it over with. When she saw Little Treasure lying by the bed, she picked her up and took her downstairs. Stroking her and nuzzling her fur she whispered, 'Are you missing Lucy too. Where's Blanche then?' Gently setting her down on the floor, she began pouring cat biscuits into Little Treasure's bowl. It was then she noticed that Blanche hadn't touched her breakfast. That was strange because Blanche liked her food and she should be looking for something to eat by now.

Gulping down a few biscuits as quickly as she could, Little Treasure meowed loudly and rushed back upstairs to Lucy's room. Puzzled, Clare followed her. Little Treasure sprang onto the bed, accidentally landing on Blanche's head. Clare heard a faint grunt from under the duvet; she pulled it back and gasped as she saw Blanche. It was obvious that Blanche was not well. Her eyes were closed and she was hardly breathing. Clare decided that she had better not move her. Hoping that she could coax her to eat or drink something, she went downstairs and brought her a bowl of water and a sachet of her favourite food. She placed the two bowls on the bed, but Blanche wasn't interested.

Clare was too worried to leave her so she knelt by the bed, talking to her until she eventually heard Andrew's car returning. Blanche heard it too and lifted her head. With an effort, she pulled herself out of the duvet and tried to stand. For a fleeting moment, she thought Lucy was with him. But only one set of footsteps came through the front door. Only one set of footsteps was coming up the stairs and it didn't take her long to work out that they belonged to Andrew. Lucy had not come back home.

Dropping her head in despair, she sank back down on the bed again. When Andrew appeared in Lucy's bedroom doorway, Clare flung herself into his arms. Between shuddering sobs, she tried to tell him how worried and upset she was. Not only because Lucy had left home but also because of what they had done to Blanche. Blanche was fretting and it was all their fault. They hadn't even thought about Blanche missing Lucy when she went to university. What had they done?

Clare and Andrew watched helplessly, as Blanche became weaker and weaker through the night. She refused to eat or drink anything. In the morning, Clare decided to phone the vet. When he came to the house and saw Blanche, he shook his head and talked about taking her to his hospital. Clare and Andrew told him that they did not think it would be a good idea to move her to a strange place, it might distress her even more.

As the days passed, Blanche sank further and further into a dark place; she had strange dreams and heard strange voices. Now she was dreaming about Lucy and her voice sounded so real. In the dream, Lucy was kneeling by the bed. She was cradling her in her arms and whispering, 'I'm sorry, I'm so sorry.' Blanche opened her eyes but it was a bit difficult for her to focus because she was so frail. This must be her last and most perfect dream because she thought she could actually see Lucy. She could even smell her and feel her long, curly hair falling over her face the way it always did when she cuddled her. Suddenly, she stiffened and caught her breath. This was no dream. Lucy was here with her. Could it be true?

Yes, yes, it was true. Blanche snuggled her head into Lucy's body and weakly wrapped her front paws around her arm. She knew that she wasn't strong enough to stand, but she was strong enough to meow a soft 'Hello'. Lucy whispered 'Hello' back and held her close for a long time. After a while, she put a dish of food in front of her and, at last, Blanche began to eat. Everyone smiled and took it in turns to stroke her. They knew that she was going to be fine now.

Little Treasure wasn't very happy about the way things turned out. She had hoped that she was going to be the centre of attention. Lucy and Blanche were going to be out of the picture and she was going to be the most pampered cat in the Close. Instead, her mother hadn't left and everyone was fussing over her. Little Treasure felt as if she had really missed out and wanted to yell, WHAT ABOUT ME?

She watched as Lucy lovingly tucked the duvet around Blanche. She heard her murmuring in her ear, 'You have a little nap now.' When Blanche's breathing settled down and became regular, the family quietly tiptoed out of the room. Little Treasure didn't follow them. Although she was feeling jealous of her mother, she didn't want to leave her. She stayed by the bed and watched as her mother snuggled down. Then, Blanche raised her head and softly called Little Treasure's name. Little Treasure leapt onto the bed and Blanche made a space for her in the duvet. They wrapped their front paws around each and smiled.

Of course, Little Treasure wanted to be admired and petted by the cats and people in the Close. But there was only one cat who really loved her and made her feel safe and that was her mum. Of course, she was glad she hadn't gone away and left her. After all, her mum would carry on being the most important cat in the area and, in a way, that made her important too.

Blanche never found out exactly what had happened when Lucy went away or how she came back. To be honest, she didn't really want to know. Eventually, she did hear talk of Lucy being lucky because she had been able to change universities and live at home. But all Blanche really cared about was that Lucy had not left her. Lucy had come back to the Close to be with her until The Great Cat God of Forever Sleep came and told her that her Cat Pledge of Loyalty to Lucy had come to an end.

On the night that Lucy came back, the full moon shone down on the Close and it illuminated the bowed branches of the chestnut tree. From the shadows underneath them the soft sound of praying could be heard. With a bowed head, The Wise White

Cat was sitting on his haunches holding his front paws together. He was chanting the same words over and over again. 'Great Cat God of Destiny, I honour you and your mystical power. Great Cat God of Destiny, I am humbled by your forgiveness for my failures. Great Cat God of Destiny, I thank you for bringing Lucy back home.' Finally, he stood on his back legs and stretched his body to its full length. Lifting his face to the moon, he opened his mouth and yowled a special yowl of worship to his God and his yowl was heard by every cat in the Close throughout the night.